VIRGIN PRINCESS'S MARRIAGE DEBT

VIRGIN PRINCESS'S MARRIAGE DEBT

PIPPA ROSCOE

MILLS & BOON

First published in Great Britain 2019
by Mills & Boon, an imprint of HarperCollins*Publishers*
1 London Bridge Street, London, SE1 9GF

Large Print edition 2020

ISBN: 978-0-263-08916-5

MIX
Paper from
responsible sources
FSC™ C007454

This book is produced from independently certified
FSC™ paper to ensure responsible forest management. For
more information visit www.harpercollins.co.uk/green.

Printed and bound in Great Britain
by CPI Group (UK) Ltd, Croydon, CR0 4YY

For Sharon Kendrick.
Without your amazing,
encouraging, supportive advice
I would never have finished this book.
You are a true Modern queen!

PROLOGUE

THEO LOOKED AT his watch again. She was late. This wasn't the first time they'd snuck out of the impossibly expensive Swiss boarding school at night, but this time felt different. She'd said that she had a surprise for him and he couldn't for the life of him figure out what that might have been.

Knowing Sofia, it could be anything. She was like that. Impulsive, reckless, often secretive… and most definitely alluring. It had taken Theo a good long while to believe that she wasn't like the other kids at this school. This school that he hated.

He wasn't naïve. He knew attending a school this reputable was a thing he could not take for granted—even if at every single turn the other students tried to make him believe that he shouldn't be there. It hadn't taken him long to realise that he was not wanted, the poor illegitimate scholarship kid polluting their air.

He almost shrugged a shoulder at the train of his thoughts. Why should here be any different to the way he had been brought up in Greece, with his mother's family?

The teachers were hardly any better than the students. If there was something to be blamed, it would be his fault. But they couldn't deny his grades. At seventeen he already had scholarship offers at some of the world's leading universities and there was nothing he'd do to jeopardise that. No, Theo Tersi was going to make damn sure that he never had to return to his mother's family vineyards in the Peloponnese. He would be a banker, something in finance. He wanted an office, like his mother's current employer who had paid for his education here. He would never scrabble around in the dust like his uncles and cousins—the ones who had taunted him since his birth. So, no. He wouldn't fight back against the bullies here. He couldn't. Not without risking everything he'd worked so hard for. Because he wanted more. For his mother, for himself. He wanted never to feel the sting of rejection and shame and hunger... And once he got out of this school, once he finished university, he would make sure that no one would taunt him again.

He looked again at his watch, the round white face gleaming in the moonlight. Where was she? Sofia was usually already waiting for him. He looked around. The night seemed almost unnaturally still, as if it were holding its breath, as if in expectation…

And he felt it too. That anticipation, the moment when he would see Sofia emerging from whatever shrub she was hiding behind. He still had to pinch himself sometimes. Never quite sure if he could really believe that someone like her would really be interested in someone like him. But tonight…he was going to tell her. Tell her that he loved her. That he wanted her to be with him when he left for university…that he wanted the life they had often talked about having in the last six months. Because somehow she'd worked her way through the anger and distrust he'd first met her with, she'd broken down the barriers all the taunts and cruel tricks the other students had thrown his way.

She had been the one bright thing in his days at school over the last few months. For so long his life had simply been about him and his mother, doing whatever it took to get through the day. He'd hated how his mother was treated by her family…because of him, because of the father he'd never met, and never wanted to. The move from Greece to Switzerland had been a fresh start for them both—the opportunity at this school one almost unimaginable for a housekeeper and her son.

And no matter what people threw at him, Theo was determined to bide his time here, knowing that it would get him to where he wanted to be. But the moment he'd first seen Sofia…the way her oceanic blue eyes had sparkled with mischief, the way his heart had kicked and thrashed, as if for the first time, when her gaze collided with his he had found something more from life than just lessons and determination. And it had never stopped, that heart thumping. He felt that same way every single time he saw her.

She had this air about her, as if nothing bad could ever touch her. And it was addictive. He leant into it every chance he could get. But he worried about her, wanted to protect her from herself even. If the school prankster was caught pulling another stunt, the headmaster had been clear—they would be expelled. He doubted they'd ever guess it was the sweet, innocent-looking blonde angel she appeared to be. But he couldn't deny that it was exactly that strange, thrilling combination of innocence and recklessness that had first drawn him to her.

He wasn't quite sure what it was, but there was also a deep desperation within her. Some kind of urgency that called to him, to his feelings for her...his love. She hadn't said much about her family, dropping little breadcrumbs of information about a loving but strict home that stifled the freedom Sofia loved so much. It certainly didn't sound like something that he would run from. But there would be time to uncover the secrets she held. There would be the rest of their lives.

That he was another of her secrets, he hated... It came far too close to the way he thought his father must have felt in order to flee from their village the same night of his birth. As if there was something about Theo that was shameful or embarrassing somehow.

A noise in the bushes off to his left startled him, his heart racing, knowing that it wouldn't settle until he saw her.

'Tersi. I was told I'd find you here.'

Instead of Sofia's softly accented Iondorran tones, fear sliced through his high hopes as the voice of his headmaster cut into the night.

He didn't move. Not a muscle. His heart dropped, sickness and nausea an instant reaction to being caught doing something he shouldn't be doing. But greater than that was his concern for Sofia.

'What's going on?' Theo ventured to the man who had never liked him.

'What's going on is that I now have my prankster. Did you really think that I would allow my car, *my car*, to be put onto the roof of the sports hall and take no action?'

Theo was shaking his head. 'I don't know anything about that, sir, honestly.'

The grim look of determination on the older man's face told Theo that he wasn't believed. Not for a second. Panic began to set in then.

'Where's Sofia?'

'The princess has returned to Iondorra.'

'Princess? What are you talking about?' Theo demanded, any hesitation overruled by his confusion.

'She didn't tell you?'

'Tell me what? Sir, please—'

'Did you really think that a princess would be interested in...?'

The man must have seen the look on Theo's face, the one he knew had descended as quickly as the fury had whipped within his chest. If there was even a moment of pity, or hesitation from the headmaster, Theo didn't see it.

'Well, it's done. She's gone. And you, skulking around in the shadows waiting to see the effect of your handiwork, will regret the day you pulled this last prank.'

'Mr Templeton, I didn't do anything to your car,' Theo said, desperately trying to hold on to his temper.

'No? Then why is your school scarf wedged underneath the wheel arch of my Mini Cooper?'

'I have no—'

Horror hit Theo hard and fast. The last time he'd seen his scarf he had been looping it around Sofia's neck as she shivered in the cold winter's sun. Sofia had lied to him? She was a princess? It was impossible. But as Theo was marched back to the headmaster's office, his quick mind ran over the images that shifted like a kaleidoscope in his memory. Every inter-action, every conversation, every kiss and his stomach turned. Each memory played to the sound of taunts he had never risen to. The cries and jibes of students belittling him for his hum-ble beginnings—ones he had taken because this school had been his ticket out. His way to rise up, no matter what people said or did. But Sofia? She was the one who had wanted to keep their relationship a secret. She was the only one who had known where he would be that night. She was the one who had said she had a surprise for him. She was the one who had been pulling the pranks all this time, and had finally left his scarf at the site of the latest one. Had it all been a ruse? Had she spent the last six months priming him to be the patsy? The fall guy to take the blame for her pranks? Was that why he'd doubted her in the begin-ning, because somewhere deep down he had known it was all lies? Had she really been the cruellest of them all, to make him fall in love with her, when he should have known better?

He was going to be expelled. He was going to lose everything. Because of her.

CHAPTER ONE

Paris...ten years later

PRINCESS SOFIA DE LORIA of Iondorra looked out across the Parisian skyline as the sun began its slow summer descent over the rooftops and cobbled streets of Europe's reportedly most romantic city. The irony was not lost on her. Tonight she would meet the man she would spend the rest of her life with. Not that romance had anything to do with it. No, that was the domain of Angelique—the practical, determined matchmaker who had been employed for that express purpose.

The hint of jasmine that settled around the room of the luxurious hotel near the Sixth Arrondissement from some invisible air dispenser was nothing like the real thing and Sofia longed to return to her palace in Iondorra. Although she did appreciate the soft white and gold tones of the room and, casting a look to the king-sized bed, her heart lurching, she felt desperate to throw herself amongst the soft pillows and deep comfort offered by the impossibly thick duvet. She had been away too long, immersed in diplomatic duties unruffling more than a few feathers caused by her father's recent and increasing absence from the world's stage. More and more, she found that she just wanted to go home.

She pulled her gaze from the incredible view of the Jardin de Luxembourg and paced towards the larger seating area of the stunning suite. Only yesterday she had been in Prague, two days before that, it had been Istanbul. Her body moved oddly within the costume for that evening's masquerade ball—the full corset holding her back straight and pushing her breasts against the gentle arc of the low, sweeping neckline. She felt confined by it, not that it was an unfamiliar feeling to Sofia. The bustle of material behind her, falling into a wide golden train, made her feel as if she were pulling the weight of more than just her, and Sofia couldn't help but think that it somehow fitted that evening.

The masquerade ball being held to celebrate

the birthday of one of Europe's minor royals had presented the perfect opportunity to meet her three would-be suitors without attracting the notice of the world's press, or the intrigue of the very royal and rich society that had been waiting with bated breath to see who the Widow Princess would marry next.

A sliver of pain twisted through her heart as she recalled the description favoured by the international press so much that it had almost become part of her title. Princess Sofia of Iondorra—the Widow Princess.

Every time it was mentioned it was accompanied by images of her in mourning, her pale skin harsh against the depth of the black clothes she had worn to honour her husband. Four years. Antoine had been gone for four years. The familiar sense of grief, softened only slightly over the years, edged around her heart. Theirs might not have been a love match in the truest sense, but Antoine had been her friend, her confidant. He had known about her father's illness and helped shield it from the world. He had supported her through their brief marriage as she adjusted to the reality that she would be queen much sooner than anyone had ever expected.

She missed his quiet support and understanding and once again felt the strange sense of bafflement that had met the news of his shockingly unexpected death at a charity car race. The footage of the six-car pile-up in Le Mans had shocked nations, but only devastated one. Because only Antoine's life had been lost.

But she could not afford to indulge in her grief. Not tonight. Antoine, more than anyone, would understand why she needed to remarry for the good of her country. Her father's illness had deepened in the last few months, and, whether she liked it or not, the council was right. If the news of his illness broke while she was still considered the Widow Princess, then the future of her country would be in serious jeopardy. With a fairly inexperienced prime minister forced into making difficult austerity measures, the monarchy was the only stability and security the people believed in. And the only way Iondorra would survive the impending announcement of her father's diagnosis was if they had some hope for the future—a fairy-tale marriage heralding the next generation of royals.

It hadn't been Antoine's fault that they'd not conceived during their four-year marriage. They had tried a few times, but even Sofia had been forced to admit that neither had been able to bring themselves to actually consummate their marriage. And she knew why. Only once had she experienced a chemistry, an attraction that had been at once all-consuming, that had seemed almost to threaten her very sanity. And it hadn't been with Antoine.

It hadn't taken long before her husband had started to look elsewhere for the pleasure that she simply could not offer him. He'd been so devastatingly discreet and quiet about it all. Every now and then he would disappear for a few days, and return with some impossibly expensive gift, offering it to her with eyes that could never meet her gaze. It hadn't angered her, torn her up inside the way it should have done. Instead, all she'd been able to feel was so very sad for the man she cared for like a friend, like a brother, to be trapped in the same cage she was caught within. Duty. A passionless marriage.

And here she was again, on the brink of yet another one. Wasn't the definition of madness doing the same thing over and over again, expecting a different result?

'Are you ready?' Angelique's voice came from somewhere behind her.

'For the royal equivalent of speed dating?' Sofia asked. 'Yes,' she said, answering her own question, all the while shaking her head to the contrary.

Angelique smiled, the movement softening her features into something more relatable than the fierce businesswoman persona she usually adopted.

'Are you sure this is what you want? We can always cancel, find some other way...'

'Are you trying to do yourself out of a commission? That doesn't seem very wise.'

Angelique cocked her head to one side, quite birdlike. 'My finances are perfectly secure, I assure you, Your Highness. And, as you have requested the utmost secrecy, then so would be my reputation. You *do* have a choice, Sofia.'

But they both knew that was a lie. Sofia looked to the window again, as if it were an exit route, as if she could fly to it and escape from what was about to happen. Because some-how, in some way, Sofia simply couldn't shake the feeling that, after tonight, her life would drastically change.

Yes, she'd have met and chosen the man she would marry, but it felt bigger than that. It felt as if she were on a precipice but that she couldn't see the edge. And it made her angry. Angry for all the sacrifices she had already made, and the ones she could continue to make in the future. As if a summer thunderstorm had zapped her with a lightning strike, coursing white-hot heat through her veins. But where once she would have vented her anger, her fear, all this impossible-to-express energy, Sofia had to fight it. Princesses didn't get angry. They got married.

'Okay,' Angelique said finally as if, too, sensing there was no going back. 'So, would you like the motivational speech now, Your Highness?'

Sofia couldn't help but smile at the gentle humour in Angelique's tone. It felt like years since someone had laughed with her. It *had* been years.

'What would you like? *Braveheart*-style,

Beyoncé *Run the World*, or something *à la* Churchill?'

Sofia let a small, sad laugh escape from her lips. 'I'll forgo the attempt at a Scottish accent, I think. I don't suppose you have anything just for me?' she asked, instantly hating the sense of vulnerability her words evoked.

'I do,' Angelique said, locking serious eyes with hers. 'You will be a great queen. You will care for Iondorra with as great a sense of purpose as any who have gone before you. You will rule her with love and duty and sacrifice, but all of that will ensure Iondorra's longevity amongst the world's greatest nations. And you will do it with a man at your side who will love, honour and protect you in a way that allows *you* to protect *your* country. You, Your Highness, are a force to be reckoned with and my wish for you is that you find a man worthy of that. These three suitors are perfect candidates. They understand your duty, your role in life, and are willing and able to support you in that. And now it is time.'

'To go to the ball, Fairy Godmother?'

'No, Sofia,' Angelique said gently. 'To remove Antoine's ring.'

Sofia's fingers flew to the wedding band around her fourth finger. It felt as sacrilegious to remove it, as much as it was easy for her to do so. Antoine would have understood. She placed the simple wedding band she had worn for eight years on the dressing table and felt a little bit of her past slip away from her grasp.

As Angelique left the room, Sofia returned her watchful gaze to the Parisian rooftops. For just a moment, she had fallen under the spell of the other woman's words, grateful for them, thankful. But that positive determination she had felt fizzing in her veins had disappeared with Angelique's departure. And for the first time in a while, she let the façade drop and allowed the feel of exhaustion to sweep over her. Her father's deterioration had increased in the last few months and propelled the need for the one thing she'd been putting off for several years. The cost of keeping her father's illness a secret had been a great one to pay, but one that she would do again and again. Because the people of Iondorra needed security.

She thought of her little European principality, cradled in between France, Switzerland and northern Italy. The country that she was to rule, protect as if it were her child. The country that, ever since she was seventeen and had been whisked away from her boarding school, she had been trained to protect, ruthlessly sculpted to become the perfect princess.

And then, as always following these moments of weakness, came the inner strength that saw her match even the strongest heads of state at the tables of European negotiations. She, and Iondorra, had no time for selfish, moping thoughts. She'd put those things aside a long time ago. Just as she'd put aside the thoughts of her own happy-ever-after.

Poor little princess, an inner voice mocked, sounding very much like that of a young man she'd long ago loved. A young man she'd been forced to leave behind, lie to, and a man she very much refused to think of now.

She glanced at the embossed invitation, smiling at how the gold detail of the lettering matched the soft golden yellows of the corseted Victorian-era dress she wore, the crinoline underskirt as heavy as a crown.

For so long she'd been cast as the Widow Princess, it had begun to feel as if she'd lost herself. Not that it mattered. The only thing of true importance was Iondorra. And attending the masquerade ball was just the next step towards the throne.

Each of the three men had been carefully vetted and would, in their own ways, be perfectly acceptable candidates for their role as husband. So there she was, in Paris, dressed up and ready to find the man she would spend the rest of her life with. And if she'd once thought she already had, then it didn't matter. Such fanciful daydreams were for others. Real princesses didn't have the luxury of Prince Charmings.

Theo Tersi scanned the expanse of the large Parisian ballroom, took a breath and instantly regretted it. Where he had expected to taste the hint of satisfaction at the thought of what tonight would bring, the only thing on his tongue was the cloying and competing scents of the perfume adorning the many women in the room. It was an assault on his olfactory system and he was half tempted to retreat and preserve that much-needed function. When he would think back to this moment in the months to come, he would wonder if it had been some kind of cosmic sign to turn back. To think again.

But right now, there was no turning back for Theo.

'All right, I'm here,' grouched the exiled Duke of Gaeten.

'You don't need to sound so pleased about it,' Theo said absently, still scanning the faces in the ballroom for the one that he wanted. No, *needed*. 'Surely the great Sebastian Rohan de Luen is not bored in the face of all this as yet untouched potential?'

'Hah,' his friend almost spat. 'You think me jaded?'

'No, as I said. Bored. You need someone to challenge you.'

'And you need to walk away from this madness before it gets us all into trouble.'

Theo turned and cast a look over his closest friend, the only person who had been there for him when his world came crashing down for the second time. They had been in the middle of a business meeting—Theo soliciting a deal that would see the wine from his vineyard served at Sebastian's Michelin-starred hotels scattered across the globe—when he had received the call from the hospital informing him of his mother's admittance and diagnosis. The bottom had literally dropped out of his world, and Sebastian? Had chartered a private plane to return him to Greece and, rather than simply letting that be the end of it, had contracted Theo's vineyard to his hotels. It had been the only thing that had saved Theo and his business from the wolves—but more importantly it had provided him with enough capital to pay for his mother's healthcare. Without that contract, he would have lost the vineyard, would have lost the roof over his and his mother's heads, and possibly would have lost his mother. And Theo had never forgotten it, and would never. Their relationship had quickly grown from business to brotherhood and, despite the awful foundation of its start, he wouldn't regret it. It had been his salvation in the years since.

But, throughout that dark time, Theo had only seen one face, one person to blame, one person who had lied to him, set him up to take full blame for her actions, and had singlehandedly ruined his life. Had it not been for her, he would have finished his education—would have attended one of the finest universities the world had to offer, and would have been able to provide his mother with more, with better. He would never have been in a position where he could have lost it all. And that fear, the fear of nearly losing his mother, had changed him, had transformed his DNA. Never again would he be the naïve youth he had once been. Never again would he be that *innocent*.

Sofia was the origin point of the change in the course of his life, one that had only exacerbated his mother's later illness. He hadn't been surprised when the doctor had explained that the stresses of the last few years had taken their toll on his mother's already weak heart. The shock of losing her job after his expulsion, the struggle of the following years... Had he not met Sofia, he would never have lost everything he'd held within his grasp—the opportunities, the chances he had been given to be and do better than either he or his mother could have ever expected. Naïve and foolish, he had believed every single one of Sofia's lies before she disappeared, making a mockery of all those words of love, of a future she would never give him—could never have been able to give—when he finally discovered the truth about her.

Oh, he had thought her to be so different to the cruel students of the international boarding school his mother's employer had sponsored him to attend, but at least they had owned their cruelty. No—Sofia's had been worse, because she had hidden her betrayal until the last moment, she had purposefully set him up to take the blame for her reckless actions and he had been expelled.

And the shame he'd felt when he realised he had lost it all? The anger that had coursed through his veins when he realised her words, her touches had been nothing more than a game to be played by a bored and spoilt princess? It had been nothing compared to the moment where his heart had shattered into a thousand pieces. The moment he'd seen the announcement of her engagement. To be betrayed by someone he had…he could no longer bring himself to say the word. He forced his thoughts fiercely away from reflections that would only see him lose his temper. And if anything was to be lost tonight, it couldn't be that.

'I spent years—*years*—watching and waiting

to see if I would lose this...need for vengeance.' He had thrown himself into any willing woman he could find in an attempt to erase the memory of her. He hadn't managed to turn his tastes to the blonde hair that seemed dull and lifeless in comparison to the lustre his memories had endowed *her* with. Blue eyes seemed bland and insipid against the sparkle and shine of the strange combination of intelligence and recklessness that seemed unique only to her. Brunettes were the only way forward through those dark, hedonistic two years as he had tried and failed to satiate the wild, driving need for her... for revenge that had all but consumed him.

'Two years in which you developed a truly debauched reputation,' Sebastian said, cutting through his thoughts.

'You sound jealous.'

'I am. How on earth am I supposed to be the most notorious playboy in Europe, if you are there competing for that same title?'

Theo couldn't help but smile.

'But,' Sebastian said, his mocking gaze growing serious, 'despite all that, my sister doesn't seem to have realised that she will never have your heart.'

'I don't have a heart to give, Sebastian,' he growled, 'but I will speak to Maria. I had hoped that it might dissipate with time, but—'

'I know you do not encourage it,' Sebastian said, slinging an arm around Theo's shoulders. 'Truly. But she is still very much…'

Clearly unable or unwilling to describe the extent of Maria's infatuation with Theo, Sebastian trailed off.

'It will be done. *Kindly*,' Theo assured him.

He liked Maria, but no matter how much he resisted her somewhat naïve attempts to pursue him, nor how many headlines proclaimed him to be just as debauched as her brother, she had not been put off. Yet. Depending on how tonight would go, it could be the final nail in the coffin of her yearning for him.

Apparently appeased, Sebastian replaced his mask and turned back to the party. Following his lead, Theo took a glass of the prosecco and bit back the curse that Europe's insistence that the masses should drink the alcohol like water had clearly infiltrated this Parisian ballroom too. Yes, he made his money with wine, but his tastes ran to whisky this evening, and right now he'd give someone else's kingdom for one.

Theo took in the glamorous couples, the range of costumes that were everything from the sublime to outrageous, but never ridiculous. The sheer extravagance and money in the room saw to that. His quick mind calculated the cost of such an event. The room hire, the staff, the overpriced and frankly unpalatable alcohol being served, all of it would fund a thousand small businesses well into the next year, a fact probably not even considered by the birthday girl's family.

After he'd spent the first few years of his adult life weighing up every single decision, every single purchase, his ability to price almost anything was ingrained. Deeply. From the moment he had returned to Greece with his mother after his expulsion from school, the shame he had brought to the family who had funded his education there, the termination of his mother's employment, and the return to the people who had rejected them both ever since his conception...he had never lost the taste of bitterness in his mouth, no matter how rich, sweet or satisfying the grape or wine he produced.

After initial notoriety as the young vintner

shocking the international wine industry—
and his mother's family—with the incredible
popularity of his Greek blended wine, he had
proved himself time and time again. And despite the almost constant criticism proclaiming his success as a flash in the pan—as if it
hadn't taken blood, sweat, his mother's tears—
even after eight years in the profession, he was
still seen as the most upsetting thing to happen in the wine world since the invention of
screw-top caps. That he'd dared to produce an
award-winning blended wine rather than that of
a pure grape somehow suited his own illegitimate status. That he persevered with blended
wines seemed only to infuriate the old-school
vintners who sniffed and huffed as he dominated the market, proclaiming him a young up-
start. He didn't feel young. Especially as he cast
a frowning glance around the fancy frippery of
the masked ball in Paris. No. He just felt jaded.

None of these people would have given him
the time of day before he'd found his success,
and Theo now returned the favour, ignoring the
lascivious glances cast his way. Instead of fir-
ing his blood, they only turned him cold. If he
was honest, not since he was seventeen had he

felt the heat of passion truly stir. Desire? Yes. The arousal of attraction? Of course. But never need. Never passion. And he fiercely reminded himself that he liked it that way. Because the last time he had felt that had heralded the destruction of every hope and dream he and his mother had ever held.

And now he was on the brink of facing his demon, he had to remind himself that he was not a monster. That *he* was not as cruel as she had been. As if sensing his resolve, Sebastian turned to him with a raised eyebrow in query.

'I will give her one chance,' Theo said, forcing his eyes back to the ballroom, back to his prey. 'If she apologises for what she did, then I will walk away, no harm, no foul.' But if she didn't, then Sofia de Loria would rue the day she had crossed him and finally learn the consequences of her actions.

CHAPTER TWO

As SOFIA STEPPED away from the second of the would-be suitors with a resigned smile, she realised that she was losing hope. Neither he nor the first were right and she couldn't help but feel that she was expecting the impossible. She was the worst Goldilocks ever. But as much as she didn't want to rush into another marriage, she didn't have a choice.

She hung back around the edges of the grand ballroom, thankful that she was hidden amongst the crowds of people watching the figures making their way round the dance floor. She had dismissed her personal assistant in order to speak to the suitors alone, and relished the opportunity for the closest thing to anonymity she'd experienced in almost ten years. The fine golden leaf-like swirls of her mask tickled at the edges of her hair, but she would take that minor discomfort for the concealment it offered. It swept upward, asymmetrically, to one side, and matched the colour of her dress perfectly.

Sofia bit back a laugh as she imagined for a moment that this would be how a wallflower, found between the pages of some historical romance, felt. Both terrified and hopeful of being plucked from obscurity to dance beneath the candlelit chandeliers by the handsome prince. But hers wasn't that kind of story. No, *she* was the royal and it seemed that the second sons, or cousins—like the two previous candidates who had seemed so fine on paper—had quite definitive ideas about *their* place within *her* royal office.

She had never wanted it. Not in truth. As a child, she had hardly been perfect princess material. Her parents had despaired and sent her to boarding school, tired of having to bribe the Iondorran press to silence yet another social faux pas on their daughter's behalf. For security reasons they had all agreed to keep her royal status a secret. But for Sofia it hadn't been about a desire for protection, it had been her last attempt for something normal, to be treated like anyone else. But ultimately that had backfired in the most spectacularly painful way.

She became aware of the feeling of someone watching her. As a princess, she was reluctantly familiar with the sensation, but this was different. This *felt* different. The hairs on her arms lifted beneath the unseen gaze, and her pulse picked up at her neck almost painfully. She couldn't shake the feeling that she was somehow being sought out...*hunted*.

She cast a glance around the room to see if she could identify the source. A sea of vivid masks and incredible costumes greeted her, and she caught herself in the unconscious protective movement she hated as her hand went to soothe the phantom sensitivity at her ribs caused by that awful night a year and a half ago.

She was surrounded by people, all engaged in conversations, bodies pressed closer together by the illicit nature given to the mass by the disguise of masks and costumes, but none seemed to be looking her way.

Discarding the feeling as foolish, much like her earlier impression that somehow her life was going to change irrevocably, she searched for Angelique, who had gone to locate her final suitor, but saw no sign of either of them. As the orchestra picked up the threads of a familiar waltz a feeling of nostalgia swept over her.

She could only hold out hope for this final suitor, because without him her country would be left vulnerable and she couldn't, wouldn't, allow that to happen.

It was not her father's fault that he'd been diagnosed with early-onset dementia. But she couldn't help but feel responsible that she hadn't been ready to assume royal duties earlier to prevent the extreme financial loss her country had experienced under his unstable reign. Feel embarrassed that she had been so carefree and reckless as to need two years of strong, mindful guardianship to ensure that she wouldn't bring further damage to Iondorra as every wilful, mindless frippery was ironed out of her character. Feel that sense of guilt that the necessary secrecy of her father's ill health had continued for so long…the silence almost as painful as the disease itself. For surely if she had been a better princess, a better ruler, they wouldn't have had to indulge in this secrecy?

She thought of her mother, tucked away in the privacy of the smaller holdings of the royal family in Iondorra, imprisoned with her husband and a handful of staff and medical professionals ready to manage and care for whatever latest outpouring of anger, frustration or confusion her father experienced almost daily now.

She knew she needed to accept the grief at the loss of a man who had once been a loving father and a fantastic ruler, but she just couldn't. She had grown to almost resent the days of coherence as much as the ones where all semblance of his sanity was lost. They were the ones that she hated most. When she saw her father once again as the man who had loved her, laughed with her, despite the strict requirements he needed her to adhere to. Of course, that was before the diagnosis and her sudden and shocking departure from the international boarding school. Ever since then her life had become one solely of duty.

A waiter paused by her side, offering her a glass of prosecco. She knew that she needed to keep a clear head for this evening, but she couldn't help but clasp the fine glass stem, relishing the cool liquid as it fizzed and bubbled on her tongue.

She was just about to leave the confines of the crowd around her when the hairs on her neck lifted once again and she felt enveloped by the warmth from a body close behind her. Shocked at the proximity of the unseen figure, she breathed in, ready to turn, when the musky, earthy scent of cologne hit her and held her still. It was unfamiliar amongst the sickly sweet, almost chemical fragrance of many of the men here. He waited, as if allowing her to become familiar with his presence, before sweeping around to stand in front of her and bowing long and low. As he straightened and held a hand out to her, she took in the way the white mask disguised his face and almost smiled as his head cocked to one side towards the dance area. The gesture seeming both inquisitive and vaguely arrogant at the same time. A challenge almost, as if daring her to refuse his request.

A feeling familiar, yet so distant as to almost be heartbreaking, rose in her chest. Defiance, recklessness and something more…something almost tantalising made her reach out, made her place her hand in his, even though no word had been spoken, even though the mask he wore concealed his identity. As his fingers closed over hers and he led her towards the dance area she felt a strange sense of vertigo, reminding her of the precipice she had imagined herself upon earlier that evening.

Her thoughts were sent scattering and fleeing as the figure released her to bring her whirling around in such a way that she had to press her hand to the man's chest in order to prevent herself from crashing into him and losing her balance and breath in one move.

The warmth that greeted the palm of her hand through the thin shirt burned her, sending tingles and fire bursts across her skin and neck, raising a blush of sudden and shocking heat to her cheeks. But, as she went to pull back, his hand came down against hers, anchoring it in place. She stared at his fingers, unaccountably reluctant to see the face of her captor. The deep tan spoke of sunshine and heat, and her eyes snagged on the roughly calloused skin covering the powerful hand.

As the music began he pulled her hand away from his chest into the traditional hold for the waltz as warmth and something else, something almost dizzying, spun out from his hold at her back. The positioning was wrong—his hand too close to the base of her spine to be appropriate for strangers, almost possessive in a way that fired her blood and sent a thrill through her that settled horrifyingly low within her. But that was madness. Surely she couldn't be feeling the stirrings of desire for a complete stranger?

His hold was firm, commanding, and, God help her, she relished it, welcomed it, the need to give herself over to this one stolen moment, for someone else to take the weight of responsibility and duty that almost crippled her. Hidden by the disguise of her mask, she was convinced that this man had no idea who she was. He couldn't, because surely he wouldn't behave so daringly with a princess? And the freedom that thought offered sang in her veins. That just for this moment she could be something other than the Widow Princess. Simply Sofia—herself, a woman with nothing more on her mind than dancing with a handsome man. For despite the mask he wore, she could tell he *was* handsome. The breadth of him, the smoothness of his skin, the inherent confidence more appealing than any physique she could determine. Her heart kicked within her chest as the stranger guided her into the first steps of the waltz, and she raised her gaze, expecting to find him looking down at her intently.

But he wasn't.

She traced the angle of his neck with her eyes, the fine, straight cord powerful and determined, to a jaw that was stubbled in a way that almost wilfully challenged propriety. Treated only to his profile, she consumed every inch of what she could see, and her body reacted as if it had been starved of the sight of it. Which made no sense.

The turn of his head hid the bare section of the mask she recognised from a well-known musical, concealing much of what she could see. His eyes were focused on some distant point on the other side of the room and the heady scent of him filled her lungs as she breathed through the steps of the dance.

There was something almost cold about the way his head was turned away from her...as if, despite the intimacy of the hold, he was *forcing* himself to touch her. And suddenly she felt nauseous. As if her body had somehow tricked her, fooled her into thinking that...what? That her Prince Charming had finally come for her? As if sensing her sudden resistance, her attempt to flee before it had even registered in her mind, he tightened his embrace, all the while remaining turned away from her.

Realising the futility of escape, she used the time to observe the stranger. He was tall, at least six feet, if not more. His shoulders, though pressed back in a perfect frame for the waltz, somehow managed to crowd her in a way that made her, made *them*, feel isolated from the other couples on the dance floor. He led her almost expertly through the movements of the dance and her body's muscle memory bowed to his command. While her mind raced with outrage and confusion that she would be so ignored, so manhandled, her body soared at the unspoken dominance.

The stranger had yet to say a word to her and somehow that made this moment all the more surreal, as if they had mutually agreed that speaking would break this strange spell that he was weaving around her. She knew she should break it though, she knew she should be outraged, terrified even, but there was something…the breadth of him, the feel of his hand within hers…both strange and familiar.

She felt known by him, even if she did not

know him. She began to count down the steps to the end of the dance, recognising the cadence and swell of the music as her pulse beat within her chest in time with the waltz, in time with him.

She didn't know what to expect when the dance came to an end. Would he finally speak? Would he look at her, or would he disappear as easily as he had swept her towards the dance floor? She both longed for and resisted the end to this moment and as he brought their steps to a close, bowed, deep and low, her curtsey only half what it should be, because she had yet to be able to take her gaze from finally seeing who this stranger was.

Only when their eyes met, a sob escaped her mouth as she caught the devastating brown orbs, dark against the pure white of the mask, and she was filled with a fury and anger that stole her breath. She actually felt the single lost heartbeat caused by the jolt of recognition.

Theo Tersi.

Theo had feared that he might not recognise her here amongst the disguises and outrageous costumes of such rich company. He had lost

Sebastian to his own personal pursuits some half an hour before, and had been beginning to lose patience. It had to be tonight. It had to be now. Everything in him had been building to this moment for years. He would not let this chance pass.

In truth, it was his body that had recognised her first. The way his pulse unaccountably hitched in his chest, the way awareness had pulled from him an almost electric current that snapped and hissed across his skin. And when he finally did see her, clinging to the edges of the ballroom, he knew that he shouldn't have doubted himself. Even had he not gone to sleep each night for ten years with her face the last thing he saw, the lies and abused promises on her lips the last thing he heard, he would have known her in the dark surrounded by a thousand people. Because she shone like a beacon of pure golden light and he bitterly noted that it had nothing to do with her costume. She had looked like the stepdaughter in the Mother Holle story told to him by his mother in childhood—the one who passed beneath a waterfall of gold. Yet he knew better. She was the other sister—the one who should have been covered in tar.

He hadn't intended to lead her into the waltz, but the moment the idea struck, it wouldn't loosen its grip on his mind. He knew that she wouldn't recognise him, certainly not if he kept his head turned away from her. She probably hadn't given him a second thought since setting him up to take the fall for her pranks. Or maybe she had, laughing to herself long and hard at how she'd manipulated him, how she'd got him to do her bidding.

Holding her and not looking at her had been a sweet torture. He'd wanted to bare his gaze to her, bore into her the feelings of anger, pain and betrayal… But when he had finally met her eyes, holding them captive with his own, he'd nearly cursed. Because it was he who consumed every emotion that flickered and sparked in her sapphire-blue eyes.

After all these years he'd thought himself immune to her. He'd thought the consequences of her actions would have made him impenetrable to the insatiable desire for her…but the way her body had melted into his, the flickering of her pulse beneath his hand, mocked him as his body had claimed her in the most primal of ways. Because no matter what had passed between them, his body still wanted her, still craved her touch.

Until the jolt of recognition from Sofia that he felt against his skin, the irrefutable horror that filled her gaze.

Now she knew him.

He was about to open his mouth, when her sudden, shocking departure slammed it shut. She had picked up her skirts and was racing away from the ballroom floor, disappearing into the crowd of people. But she would not get away that easily. He saw her at the wide French doors, open to the beckoning darkness of the gardens, and a smile curved the edges of his lips.

Theo Tersi drew out his mobile phone, and as he followed her out into the night he fired off a text to the man he had waiting on standby. If she failed to offer him the apology he so very much deserved, Sofia de Loria would regret the day she had ever thought to play him.

Plunged into the darkness of the Parisian night, he stalked amongst the manicured gardens, expecting to have to hunt much more than he did, and nearly crashed into her.

'What are you doing here?' Sofia demanded, apparently satisfied that there were no longer people to overhear them as her raised voice was carried away on the night air. Her outrage struck him low in the chest.

'Why? Not used to discovering an ill-bred bastard amongst your high-society companions?'

'What?' He noticed her brow pucker in momentary confusion. 'That has nothing to do with anything.'

'No? I'd have thought your security teams would have vetted every single person here, check their DNA for their blue-blood credentials.'

'Don't be such a snob.'

Now *he* was outraged. 'How dare you accuse me of being a snob?'

'Just because it's reverse snobbery, it doesn't make it any less prejudicial.'

'You're speaking nonsense.'

'Because I disagree with you? You never did—'

'Don't. Do not talk to me of what I did or did

not do in the past,' he spat as he lifted his mask away from his face and cast it aside onto the thick emerald grass of the gardens.

He watched her almost physically bite her tongue and he used the moment to take her in. The Sofia he knew had been breathtaking, but Sofia de Loria the Princess was obscenely beautiful. Her cheeks had lost some of the softness, striking cheekbones sculpting her face to perfection. The thick plaits of golden hair wrapped around her head glowed silver in the starlight of the night sky. A high brow made even more superior with the arch of a perfect, rich, honeyed eyebrow peeking out from the top of the mask, brilliant golden furls glinting in the moonlight.

And, as always, crystal-blue eyes crackled and sparked as she tried to repress the anger she clearly felt. An anger he matched, if not exceeded. Oh, he'd had his share of beautiful women in the last two years, once he'd given himself permission to relish and enjoy the success that all his hard work had reaped. Once he'd lifted his self-imposed embargo on sensual pursuits. But no matter how many times he'd cursed her to hell and back, he'd never been able to deny Sofia's beauty.

But even in that he knew he lied to himself. It wasn't just a simple fact of her beauty. It was as if a chemical reaction had ignited within him, fizzing in his veins, urging him to reach out and touch her. Draw her to him and seek her mouth, her kiss…to feed the burning arousal he had really only ever felt with this woman. He wanted her, needed her, with every ounce of his being. But he fought it. He would *not* give in to the temptation she unconsciously offered.

Sofia felt her chest heave against the confines of the tight corset as her body struggled for an outlet for the anger and pure shock at Theo's appearance. Masked, he was impressive. Unmasked he was undeniable. Age had only honed what were already incredible features. Even in his youth he had stood heads above even the older students, and now she had to crane her neck to look up at his scowling gaze, his deep brown irises swirling like the richest espresso. His clenched jaw was dusted with a fine dark stubble as if, even in that, Theo rejected the same propriety that saw every other man there either clean-shaven or fully bearded. His straight nose created a sense of balance between the downward slashes of his cheekbones, and the night cast his proud jaw in deep shadows.

In obvious frustration he ran his hand through his thick hair and on any other man the result would have looked chaotic, but on Theo? It just made Sofia want to reach out and do the same. He was magnificent and for a second she imagined that she could reach for him, that she could draw him to her. Desire, thick and fast, rose up within her chest, even as she knew that she could not act upon it, should not feel it.

She tried not to flinch at the sound of apparent disgust as he finally turned that lethal focus of his to her, casting the entire length of her body in a glance that was anything but lazy, or accidental. No. There was purpose to this…to make her uncomfortable, and she hated that it was working.

'If you've had your fill and there's nothing else?' She refused to stand there before his assessment and be found wanting. She just couldn't. Not tonight. She still had to meet with Joachim, the third possible suitor, her last hope.

She could not stand here caught between the past and her future—it was threatening to tear her apart.

Sofia turned to leave, but his hand snuck out and caught her at her wrist. His hold deceptively gentle. The delicate ring his fingers created around her skin thrummed with repressed tension. He tugged, and she almost fell against his chest and this time she just managed to stop her hand from leaning on his chest for... balance, she told herself. Balance.

With her hand still hovering mid-air between them, she risked a glance at his face. It was so close, angled down at her, lips that once she would have delighted in now cruelly sensual and taunting her with a knowing smile. But the anger in his eyes was easier to read than her own reaction, and she welcomed it, embraced it, used it to fuel her now.

'I'm here for an apology.'

'An apology?' Sofia didn't know how he'd caused her to revert to the stammering seventeen-year-old she'd once been. More than a decade of training, diplomacy, education and learning trade negotiations and she seemed only capable of two words around this man.

She knew she owed Theo an apology…more than that. An explanation at the very least, but before she could summon the words to her lips, he pressed on.

'You doubt it?'

'No, not at all, I—'

'Do you know what I regret most? That even as I waited the first hour for you, the second, hidden amongst that ridiculous shrubbery, I didn't even doubt you. It didn't even cross my mind that you wouldn't show. I waited, like a moon-eyed calf, half drunk on love for you. Even afterwards, when the headmaster came to find me, told me of the trick *you* pulled on his car, my first concern was for you, not for myself. My fear was that something had happened to you.'

She felt shame slash across her cheeks in a dark crimson blush, painful and stinging, as if he had slapped her with his hands rather than his words. And all the wishes, wonderings and dreams of what happened to him that night were painted in stark reality by his words.

'It didn't take me long to realise, though. Realise what you had done that night and in the weeks, months leading up to it. To realise that everything you had told me was lies, *Your Highness.*'

Secrets and lies had come back to haunt her and Sofia turned her head away, but his fingers, once again seemingly gentle, but determined, found her chin, and brought her back round to face him, to see the truth written in his eyes.

'Can you imagine what it was like to realise that I had fallen in love with a fabrication? That everything I'd felt was simply the by-product of the ruse of a bored, pampered princess with nothing more to do with her time than to move people around a chessboard of her own imagination? That I was expelled because of *your* actions?'

Shock reared through her, and she stepped back as if she could distance herself from what he was saying.

'I didn't—'

'You didn't know?' he demanded harshly, his fury palpable, shaking the very air between them. 'You didn't even know?' He cursed harshly. 'You all but ensured it when you left my scarf, *my* scarf, beneath the car. Tell me, did you even think of me when you ran back to your country playing the part of the perfect princess as I was kicked out of school? When I lost the scholarships to every single university I had gained entry to? When my mother was fired and we were forced to return to her family with little more than what we could carry? I thought of you, all the while knowing that everything we had lost, every struggle we experienced, was because of your lies!'

Sofia was struck dumb by the pain his words evoked, and the truth that lay within them. She hadn't known that he had been expelled, she hadn't even remembered that she'd been wearing his scarf when she pulled the prank with the car. Because that night, in between her plan to get revenge against the headmaster and meeting Theo, her parents had come to the school and revealed that her father had been diagnosed with early onset dementia. And in that moment, the bottom had fallen out of her world.

Every thought, hope and dream she'd ever held in her heart since falling in love with Theo had flashed through her mind, while she should have been focusing on the physical and mental sentence that had been handed to her father. That the entire time her parents had patiently tried to explain what that meant, what would happen, how she would have to ascend to the throne much sooner than anyone had ever planned for, all she had thought of was him. Theo. Standing there, waiting for her to come.

She had begged and pleaded with her parents to allow her to speak to Theo. To find him where he waited for her. To tell him what was happening. But her father had been uncompromising—no one could know of his diagnosis. No one. And then they had bundled her into a car, and then a private jet, and the whole time she had felt as if she had left her heart behind.

So, no. She hadn't thought of what had happened to him after that night, because she couldn't. She just couldn't allow herself to go there. Because every time she did, what little remained of her heart fractured and shattered just a little bit more.

But she couldn't explain that to Theo. Not now. Because her father's diagnosis still had the power to rock the already shaky foundations of her precious country. Because this? This moment between them wasn't about her or what she could say to justify what had happened that night. This was about him, and God help her, but she deserved every single word, every single feeling he expressed. She needed to honour that, because it was the only thing she would ever be able to give him.

'Tell me, Sofia, did you mean any of it? The pleas you made, the plans…the future you fabricated, all the while knowing it was impossible? Punctuating lies with kisses? Untruths with touches and caresses? When did you know that you would ruin me, Sofia? Before you first spoke to me, or when you realised how easily manipulated I would be?'

'That is enough,' Sofia commanded, digging through the hurt to find some kind of strength to ward off the harshness of his words.

'Enough? I've barely even begun. *"Please take me away, Theo, I cannot return to Iondorra, Theo. Help me. Theo."'* The cruel mockery his voice made of her childhood words stung as much as the memory of her desperation to escape the confines of a royal life she had been forced to accept.

Theo knew that he had gone too far. He had said too much. Revealed too much of his own pain and heartbreak. And he hated himself for that. He saw the moment that his words hit home, the shimmer of unshed tears in her eyes more bright than any star that night. He cursed, the breeze carrying it away from them. He steeled himself against the innate sympathy welling within him, knowing better this time than to fall for her games.

'*Christós,* I didn't know you at all, did I?'

Suddenly the cord that had bound them in the past snapped, pinging away under the pressure of a decade of hurt and distance between them. And he watched, half fascinated as that royal mantle settled once more around her shoulders, leaving no trace of the young girl he had once loved. Instead, a fury stood before him, iron will steeling her spine and her body as if no soft movement had ever settled beneath her skin.

'You are right. You did not know me. You knew a child. A girl who was reckless, pulled pranks and gave no heed to the people or things about her. A pampered young woman, who knew nothing of real life, or consequences. I am sorry if that girl hurt you, caused you pain. Truly. But she is gone, living only in your memories and imagination.'

It wasn't enough. It wasn't nearly enough, her half apology. Pain reared its ugly head. Not for the loss of her, he assured himself, but the years he endured after her. The years his mother endured. They did *not* live solely in his imagination. They were etched across his heart and hands as he had clawed his way to where he stood today.

'Now, if you don't mind—'

'Off to find your next husband?'

She stilled her entire body. It was unusual for her, because everything about her contained a restless energy, its sudden and shocking absence such a stark contrast, and for a moment he could have been forgiven for thinking she'd turned to stone.

'How do you...?'

He huffed out a cynical laugh. 'Still keeping your secrets and lies close to your chest? Well, this time I've made sure that I will not fall for either. Unlike whatever poor bastard you've chosen for your next target.'

'Target?' she sighed, a scoffing sound that grated on his ears. It was too similar to the dismissive gestures of people who had thought themselves better than him. 'You know nothing, Theo. Nothing of duty, of sacrifice. Nothing of what needs to be done as a royal.'

'You think your concerns above those of mine?' he demanded.

'Yes,' she said simply. 'Yes, I do. I have to.'

'You once begged to wear *my* ring,' he said, cursing the moment of weakness that allowed his inner thought to escape his lips. 'And instead you married that insipid—'

'Do not speak of him like that,' she commanded.

'Why not? I saw the pictures. Hell, the world saw the pictures of you together. You might as well have been siblings for all the connection you seemed to share. And after his death? You were the Widow Princess who never cried, for all you may try to profess your love for him.' If it had not been so dark, Theo might have seen how Sofia paled beneath the moonlight, might have seen how much his barb had hit home. 'Tell me, Sofia, did he ever make your pulse race, your body throb with desire? Did you ever crave his touch as you professed to crave mine?'

Theo caught the gasp that fell from Sofia's lips, proving the truth of his words and enflaming the sensual web weaving between them, as if he had conjured the very reaction from her body by his words.

Anger, frustration and desire burned heavily on the air between them, and his eyes caught the rise and fall of her perfect breasts against the curve of the corseted dress she wore. Their argument had drawn them closer together, and he could have sworn he felt the press of her chest against his through the mere inches of air that separated them, thickening his blood and his arousal instantly.

'Do you remember, Sofia? What is was like between us? Or were you faking everything?' he demanded. Because somewhere, deep down, he needed to know. He needed to know if it had all been lies. Before him, Sofia swayed, caught within the same tide of desire that he felt pulling at his entire being.

Her lips parted, shining slightly as if recently slicked with her tongue, and he was desperate to taste, to touch, to consume. He needed to know if this time, with all the knowledge he now had, he would be able to taste the lies on her tongue.

His mind roared against it, but his body closed the distance between them, unable to resist the feel of her, the siren's call she seemed to pull him in with. Surely his memory had exaggerated the way she had made him feel. Surely it could never have been that incredible.

He watched her closely, the way her eyes had widened as he'd moved closer, the way she too struggled with the thick, heavy want wrapping around them both. And he saw the moment she gave in to it. Gave in to the silent demand he hated his body for making.

He gave her the space of one breath, to turn, to flee, to refuse him. He gave himself that time, to turn back, to walk away. But when her pupils widened, that breath she took a sharp inhale, all but begging him to press the advantage, to make good on his unspoken promise, he was lost to the need pulsing in his chest. Lost to the insanity of what had been, what now was, between them.

'Tell me you don't want me, don't want my kiss. Tell me, Sofia, and I'll walk away. *Lie* to me again, Sofia,' he challenged.

'I can't,' she whispered, as if hating herself for the confession.

His arm swept around her small frame, drawing her to him and him into madness as his lips descended on hers with ten years of pent-up frustration, anger and a raging need that even the sweep of her tongue against his could not appease.

Passion and desire crackled in the air as they came together, her touch as bruising as his, the almost painful clash of lips, tongues, the merciful bite of teeth that brought clarity as much as it brought confusion.

He had thought himself lost, but a small part of him whispered instead that he'd been found. Found within her, the scent of her winding around him, pulling him even deeper into the kiss. It was everything he remembered and more. His pulse beat erratically in his ears, as if in warning, but it was drowned out by the gentle, almost pleading moans she made into his mouth. But whether Sofia was begging for more or less, he couldn't tell. And that was what made him pull away.

He wrenched himself back, shocked by the intensity of what they had shared, Sofia, looking equally stunned, her mouth quickly covered by the back of her wrist, pressing their kiss to her lips or swiping it away, he couldn't tell. He needed to sever whatever hold this madness had on him and quickly.

'Now, there's the Sofia I remember.'

'You bastard,' she cried and ran from the gardens towards the safety of the ballroom.

And he knew that, for possibly the first time in any of her exchanges, she had spoken the truth. He was a bastard. Because even as he had lost himself to the kiss, lost himself to the chaotic emotions storming within his chest, his mind was moving at the speed of light.

Because now, it was too late for her. The moment Sofia had issued that half-mustered apology had sealed her fate as surely as the shutter on the camera of the paparazzo Theo had hired to capture the moment of her compromise.

He let loose a bitter laugh. He had hoped that an image of them in a heated argument would do damage enough, but a kiss? So much better for his plan of revenge.

Yes. Sofia de Loria would very much regret the day she had ever thought to play him the fool.

CHAPTER THREE

*Widow Princess Caught in Clinch with
Wine Playboy!*

*From Widow Princess to
Scandalous Princess in One Kiss!*

*Widow Princess Tames Bad Boy
of the Wine Industry!*

THE HEADLINES SCREAMED in Sofia's mind, punctuated by exclamation marks that struck almost physical blows as she threw down the collection of newspapers unceremoniously handed to her by the royal council earlier that day. She peered through the window of the car and cast a glance up and down one of Monaco's most famous streets. The light illuminating the Plaza del Casino de Mónaco caused the water feature in the centre to sparkle in the night like a thousand diamonds.

And each and every glint scratched against her already frayed nerves and temper.

It wasn't the fact that she had been captured in a kiss with one of Europe's most notorious playboys, and splashed across the front pages for the world to see. It wasn't even the fact that the morning after the party, Joachim—her third and last hope for a fiancé—had regrettably informed Angelique that he could no longer consider matrimony with Sofia.

It was the fact that Theo Tersi—notorious womaniser—had refused to comment. And he *always* commented. By neither confirming nor denying their speculative questions, he had served only to inflame the rabid press. The Iondorran privy council had further tied her hands and refused to allow a statement to be issued by the royal communications office in a desperate act of blind ignorance, wilfully hoping that it would all 'blow over'.

But she knew better. Because the sneaking suspicion that had begun the first moment she'd seen the awful photographs had grown into a living, breathing belief that Theo Tersi had somehow managed to orchestrate this whole disaster. The birthday party in Paris had been under a strict press embargo, the girl's family having sold the rights for images to *Paris Match*. Furthermore, the only photos surfacing from that night were of them—no other guests—despite the fact that Sofia was aware of at least three front-page headline-worthy incidents. In the last three weeks she had stopped wondering how and instead focused on the why.

She bit back a distinctly unladylike growl as she exited the dark diplomatic-plated sedan, remembering how she had held herself that night as her body trembled after their conversation, after their kiss, as it shook at how he had weakened her. For the hours following, her body left overly sensitised, she had found herself pressing her fingers to her mouth as if in denial or longing, she couldn't tell, and no matter how much she wished it the low, aching throb between her legs and in her chest had both shocked and terrified her. She had allowed herself that night to feel, to ache, to want. But in the morning when she had seen the headlines, something within her had turned to steel. Sofia dismissed the guards she usually travelled with. She did not want an audience for what was about to happen.

She cast a glance up and down the stunning architecture of the buildings gathered around Monaco's famous gambling district. She had never been anywhere like it. People filled the streets, couples holding hands, groups of men stalking the bars and cafes brimming with tourists and celebrities. Their excitement was infectious, but she resisted the instinct to relish in their levity, instead clinging to her incredulity that Theo would do something so...so...

Theo had resisted every single attempt she had made to contact him. Email, telephone, text message...she had dismissed the idea of carrier pigeon as ridiculous. In the last two days he had repeatedly posted images of himself on Twitter at some of the many casinos in Monaco, and finally, just an hour ago, she had located this club as his current place of residence, if the latest Victoria's Secret model to hit the headlines was to be believed.

Two blondes, two Doms and two Ts. Lol.

Lol. Honestly. Sofia had barely repressed the acidic taste of bile at the back of her throat the moment she saw the accompanying obligatory selfie of two beautiful blondes, two bottles of

Dom Perignon and 'TT', aka Theo Tersi, grinning in the background as if he was purposefully taunting Sofia. Which he was.

Clearly less than two hundred and eighty characters were needed to explain the models' ecstasy, and the fact they had snared Theo's legendarily short attention span.

She knew that Theo wasn't naïve or stupid. He must have known that every single indecent headline following the publication of their kiss nearly three weeks ago now would take her down with him. She knew that this was an act of revenge, knew that in his mind she most definitely deserved it. And in a very small, very quiet part of her own mind, she feared that he might be right. But right or wrong had no place here. She needed to get him to issue a denial so that she could do whatever damage limitation was required and press forward with her hopes to find a forgiving fiancé.

Her heartbeat thrummed beneath the thin silk top and jeans she had chosen with the express purpose of blending in. Her aim was to get in, get him to agree and get out, without being spotted. In her youth, she had achieved much greater things under the radar. Surely this would be possible?

Her inner voice mocked her naivety, while her desperation drove her forward.

She reminded herself that no one would be looking for her here. It was the first time in nearly ten years that she'd been outside amongst people without the trappings of her royal status and she was slightly fascinated and slightly sad.

Sofia couldn't help but wonder what her life would have been like had her father not become ill. Yes, she still would have ascended to the throne, but could she have had some time? Time to explore a little fun, or even herself just a little...*more*? Would she have found some enjoyment in life in a way she could never do now? Not that she would ever have been able to fritter away money on a hand of cards, or tweet mindlessly using emojis and take selfies with any number of handsome men.

If her father hadn't come to find her that night, would she have risked it all and found a way to be with Theo as she had often dreamed? No matter how hard she tried to imagine what would have happened had she met him behind the shrubs at their boarding school, rather than the headmaster who must have been sent by her father, she just couldn't. Was that because it could never have truly happened as she had once told herself? Or because she had spent years repressing those exact thoughts and desires for far too long? She could no longer say.

Still, the Theo that she fell in love with all those years ago was now long gone. There had been no trace of him in the eyes of the man who had mocked her so cruelly. Who had taunted her, teased her into furious, anger-filled words in the Parisian garden just three weeks ago. And if there had been traces of him only in the kiss he stole from her, she chose to ignore it.

The large security guard beside the entrance to the club gave her a cursory glance and allowed her to pass through the doors into the dark, cavernous chamber beyond. Music assaulted her ears, and she blinked against the chaotically strobing light throbbing in time with a baseline she felt buzz through her skin and bone to the soft inside of her.

She shouldn't be doing this. She should just let someone else confront Theo, but she knew—instinctively—that this was what he had wanted.

As if he had planned everything down to the finest detail and only her presence would do.

Sofia brushed aside her concerns, her fears, and scanned the chaotic mass of people on the dance floor. No matter how hard she tried, she couldn't imagine Theo amongst the thriving group. No. He was far too voyeuristic for that. She remembered the feel of his gaze upon her skin at the Parisian ballroom. Remembered the feel of being hunted by a predator purposefully choosing when best to strike.

Her gaze finally took in the raised area of the club, an entire glass-fronted section roped off and guarded by another large, dark-suited man. She caught sight of the blonde model she recognised from the tweet, and, sure enough, Theo was sitting with one arm draped around her, the other draped around the thin shoulders of the other, the only difference in the scene being the additional upturned bottle of champagne beside the other two. Either the staff were very slow at tending to the tables in this club, or Theo was enjoying showing off his power and wealth. Sofia very much leaned towards the latter.

She made her way towards the large, suited man, and when she tried to pass he thrust out a meaty arm to block her. Shocked, she very nearly uttered the famously awful words, *Do you know who I am?*, but just managed to prevent herself. She was here incognito and she had not the first idea of how to get around the man. She had no experience in these situations, no idea what was required, as usually her security handled every single small thing…but she had dismissed them. Boarding school had been the last time she'd been allowed her freedom and since her return to Iondorra she hadn't exactly been out 'clubbing'.

Did she offer him money? she wondered, then belatedly realised she didn't have any. And even if she had, Sofia had no idea how much would have been appropriate. She could have given the man a year's salary, or not even enough to buy milk. Suddenly feeling completely out of her depth, she felt the sting of tears pressing against the backs of her eyelids and blamed Theo Tersi wholeheartedly. She had not cried once since the night of the debutante ball when she and her mother had spoken. When she had realised there truly was no other option but to assume the throne and marry her childhood friend, Antoine. But in the three weeks since

Theo had stormed into her life and turned it upside down, she felt as if she were only a breath away from it at all times.

Suddenly he appeared at the top of the stairs behind the bouncer, towering over her like an avenging angel, and she hated the way that her pulse instantly kicked at the sight. She pushed away the thoughts of how she had reacted to the kiss that night, with all the wanton, suppressed desire of ten years of need and yearning that she had refused to acknowledge. The photographer had caught the exact moment that she had clung to him as if her life depended on it, and the memory brought a furious blush to her cheeks even now.

She took in the sight of Theo's broad shoulders filled out from youth with powerful masculinity, dark hair artfully messy—or at least she hoped it was by design and not the hands of either of the models he was currently parading about. She bit down on the thread of shocking jealousy unfurling in her chest, and replaced it with anger as Theo growled the phrase, 'Let her come.'

It sounded more like the taunt of a battle cry than permission to enter some private section of a club. He'd turned his back on her before she'd taken the first step, and by the time she'd reached the top of the stairs he was nestled in between the two women once again.

She stood before the three of them, separated by the depth of a table with half-filled glasses and empty champagne bottles.

'Can we talk?' she shouted over the loud music.

He placed a hand to his ear, and simply shrugged in confusion as if the blasted man hadn't heard what she'd said.

'I said—' she shouted, only to realise that a sudden lull in the music had carried her voice far and wide over the private section of the club.

The two models snickered into their hands and Theo's smirk made her utterly convinced that he'd known that would happen.

'I said,' she tried again, 'can we talk?'

He waved a hand before her in a way more regal than any gesture she'd ever managed to achieve. He still had yet to say a word to her.

'In private?'

'Anything you have to say to me can be said here.'

Sofia wanted to snarl. She felt the deep yearning to be reckless, to act out, to do something so un-princess-like as to throw the remaining contents of the glass on the table all over his proud, defiant face. But ten years of suppressing that wild inner instinct won out. Even though she suspected he knew exactly what she wanted to do, what she would have done in the past. Unconsciously she rubbed at the old ache on her forearm, the other arm wrapping around the long since faded bruise against her ribs, while she chose and discarded what to say next.

'We have…business to discuss.'

'Sit,' he said, knowing full well the only place to sit was beside one of the two women he still had his arms around. And Sofia point-blankly refused to add to the collection of women he'd gathered about himself.

'I'll stand.'

He shrugged, once again as if it were her choice.

One of the girls leaned over and whispered in his ear, producing a high-pitched giggle from the other, and an amused grin and a nod of agreement from him as they both returned their attention to her, making it clear she was the subject of the private discussion.

It was becoming increasingly hard to hold on to the thin thread of her control. She locked her eyes on his, ignoring the two women either side of him, and waited. Because the one thing that no one had been able to remove from her in all her years of royal training was her stubbornness. So she watched and waited. She'd have stood there all night too, but he seemed to realise that, and finally dismissed the two women, who pouted and protested but ultimately removed themselves to a table further away. Not before casting her glances that Sofia was sure would have quelled lesser individuals. She had won that battle, but not the war. Not yet.

Theo called over a waitress and requested a chair for her, which was duly produced, and Sofia finally sat down opposite him.

'I see that you have dressed for the occasion,' Theo said as his gaze covered her once again from head to toe and back to her head again.

She raised an eyebrow and shrugged. 'When in the henhouse…'

'Are you calling me a hen?' he asked, full of

mock-horror. 'Pecking and scratching around for any little titbit you'd throw my way? Oh, no. I assure you, Sofia, that is not how this is going to play out.'

'For goodness' sake, Theo. It's the cock in the henhouse. You're the...' A painful blush rose to her cheeks before she could finish the sentence.

'Oh, that's adorable, sweetheart.'

'Don't call me that,' she commanded.

Theo felt the thrill of satisfaction as he watched her crystal-blue eyes storm like a Mediterranean downpour. He'd never failed to find enjoyment in teasing her. But seeing her feathers ruffled, seeing her annoyed and angry, held a bittersweet taste this evening.

Good. He wanted her angry. He wanted her annoyed. He wanted her to feel every single thread of emotion that had wrapped around his heart the moment he'd realised just how artfully she'd played and betrayed him. Because it wasn't just him that her machinations had affected. That his mother had been caught up in the fallout was untenable. So when Sofia failed to issue the apology he knew he deserved, she had sealed her fate. The photographer he had hired had done well and been paid well for his services too. Securing front-page headlines throughout the world had been exactly what Theo had wanted, knowing that it would back her into a corner. Knowing that no other royal would want to go near her after being associated with his debauched reputation. He had ignored her for weeks, knowing that it would only infuriate her more. Until yesterday, when he had begun to leave little breadcrumbs on social media of where she might be able to find him. He wanted her on his turf, he wanted her on the back foot, *needed* her to be. This was only the second step towards his utter and complete revenge. She would know the sting of humiliation, she would know the deep slice of hurt and betrayal—feelings that were so familiar to him it was as if he had been born with them— and she would know, ultimately, that she had brought it on herself.

His gaze ate up the image before him. She was wearing clothes he'd never seen her in, certainly nothing that would ever grace the style magazines she was often lauded in. The tight grey denim riding low on her hips made his mouth water, and the silky white top tucked into them was nowhere near indecent, but as it moulded to her perfect breasts, topped by thin straps, he couldn't imagine that she was wearing a bra. He would have seen the evidence of it. The low heel of the suede nude-coloured heels gave her overall appearance a conservative contrast to the barely dressed women at the club, teetering on almost death-defying stilettos.

He had imagined her monstrous over the years, every heartache added to the list of crimes she had perpetrated against him and his mother. He had imagined her begging and pleading for forgiveness, but in reality he could not deny the effect she had on him and cursed his body's weakness for her. Even now, he had to lean forward to hide the evidence of his arousal, his desire for her. The one thing that had never gone away.

Her pupils dilated at his slow perusal, and the realisation that she too was as beholden to their mutual attraction was the only balm to his ego.

'Theo—'

'Princess Sofia de Loria of Iondorra...'

This time she scowled. More like the youthful woman he had once known, and it struck him in his chest. He slowly exhaled the shock, but took great pleasure as those about them started to produce their smartphones and snap pictures of the two of them—some not even bothering to be discreet. He would not be her dirty little secret. Not this time. This time, he would make it impossible for her to walk away from him.

'You must issue a denial,' she said finally, as she tried to ignore the flashes punctuating the beginning of their exchange.

'A denial of what, Your Highness? That we kissed? I believe that is quite undeniable at this point.'

'That we are in a relationship,' she hissed beneath her breath. 'I can't have the world thinking that...'

'Thinking that you are involved with an illegitimate Greek commoner?'

'I was going to say Greek millionaire playboy.'

'Please,' he scoffed. 'It's *billionaire* playboy to you.'

She artfully raised an eyebrow.

'You can look at my financials if you doubt

it,' he replied, unable to keep the heady mixture of pride and arrogance from his voice. Everything he'd achieved, every grape, bottle, vineyard and investment, had been despite her machinations and through his own hard work. She could hardly claim the same.

'I'm not here to debate what names the press call *you*, I'm here to get you to put a stop to the ones they're calling *me*.'

He held back the smile that his lips itched to tease into. Instead, shaking his head and offering her a simple shoulder shrug, he said, '*Óchi*. No. I don't think so.'

'Why not?' she demanded incredulously.

'It doesn't suit my purposes to do so.'

'What do you want, Theo?' Suspicion darkened her eyes to a midnight-blue. A colour he remembered from his past, and he thrust the thought aside.

'I want,' he said, unfurling his large frame from the sofa beneath him, closing the distance between them in order to see the moment she realised that she was helpless, that she had no other choice… 'you to learn the consequences of your actions. I want you to learn that we mere mortals will not be as easily discarded as you seem to think.'

I want you to learn that you cannot destroy me and everything I hold dear and just walk away, he concluded silently.

'I want you to pay for the way you set me up—'

'Theo—'

He didn't even register her interruption as the wave of indignation and fury pounded in his veins, competing with the heavy base of the club's music.

'I want what you once promised me, what you once begged me for. I want you to make a truth from your lies. I want you to wear my ring.'

His eyes narrowed as Sofia failed to move a muscle, blink even. This mask that she wore, this impossibly regal poise, was different to the young woman he remembered. He had seen her desire to throw a glass of champagne over him earlier, a fit of female pique. But this? No, this was unacceptable. He didn't want poised. He wanted furious. He wanted her to feel what he felt.

'In fact,' he pressed on, now standing, towering above her, cocking his head to one side in a way that showed only disrespect, 'I don't just want you to agree. You see, your name is now entwined with mine. No one of royal pedigree would attach themselves to you in marriage, no matter how desperate they are. No one would want my seconds, my cast-offs. No one would ever choose you again. It doesn't matter how long you wait. Every time I cause a scandal—and trust me, *agápi mou*, I am more than willing to engage in as many I can find—every time I'm seen out with my next conquest, your name will be dragged down with me. Compared to whatever woman graces my bed, the speculation as to whether your poor, wounded little princess heart is breaking over my latest indiscretion will be on every single front page around the world.

'You should be happy, Sofia. You are now tied to me as securely—if not more so—than you used to pretend you wanted to be. So no, I don't want you to simply agree to be my wife. I want you to *beg*.'

Just like the way his mother had begged her employer to reconsider. Like the way she had been forced to beg her own family to take them in once again. Just like he had been forced to beg to buy the first piece of neglected land that he'd wanted to develop for his own grapes from his mother's family. So that was what Sofia would have to do now.

'I want you to beg.'

The words cut through Sofia like fire and ice.

Surely he had to be joking. There was no way they could marry. Not with all this hurt and anger between them. Not with the events of the past between them.

But she only had to look at him, take in the determined gleam in his eyes, the slightly forward bent of his body, the tense muscles of a predator that had already struck, had already cornered its prey and was now only playing, toying with it, before the poor creature was completely devoured. She was that creature. And she hated it. Hated him.

Still, just like that prey, she sought a way out.

'What do you get out of this?'

'Do you not see how this works? My wine sales will go through the roof. I may even request a royal seal,' he said again with that infuriating shrug.

'You'd tie yourself to me in marriage for the

rest of your life, just for sales?' she demanded incredulously.

'Princess, how is that any different than marrying for the good of your country?'

'But what about...' She trailed off.

'Love? Happy-ever-afters? I think we learned that lesson quite some time ago, don't you?'

She wanted to argue, to deny his words, to find some way of reasoning with him.

'You are blackmailing me? I have no choice in this whatsoever,' she said, panic rising from deep within her.

'Of course you have a choice. You can walk away, with your reputation in tatters and never see me again. Or we will marry. Give this little scandal a royal fairy-tale ending.'

Sofia knew that he meant it. Knew that he wouldn't let this go. Knew when she had fled the garden in Paris that she had taunted the lion in its cage.

'I'll need that answer now, Sofia.'

She bit back the curses, because there was definitely more than one ready to fall from her lips. There was too much to take in. He had set her up because he thought *she* had set him up? Was this really just some obscene marketing plan for his vineyard? The thoughts were crashing through her mind at lightning speed, but it was the realisation that he was right that came through loud and clear. There was no way that she would ever *not* be associated with him now. And she knew enough about him to take him at his word. He would make sure of it. No one would go near her now that she was linked with a debauched billionaire playboy. She had run out of time. Her father's recent deterioration had seen to that. The only way forward was the one he was offering. No, demanding. The one he had orchestrated and executed so perfectly.

She hated the smile that unfurled on his lips. The thrum of satisfaction she felt coming off him in waves that lapped her skin so very painfully. Sofia bit her tongue, as if her body was protesting the words that she was being forced to say.

'Theo Tersi, please. Pretty please, with a damn cherry on top. Will you marry me?'

CHAPTER FOUR

THEO DIDN'T KNOW what he'd expected, and, though it might have had to have been forced out of him with the threat of serious bodily harm, he was impressed.

The power and might of the Iondorran royal mechanisms was something to behold. Within a month of her agreement to his demand, a backstory to their sudden engagement had been constructed, non-disclosure agreements had been signed and an engagement party had been planned.

Only one hour ago, an airtight prenuptial agreement had been delivered to the suites assigned to him and his entourage in Iondorra's impressive castle.

Theo stood in the living area nestled within a turret, looking out through a slender window that displayed a view of the rolling green countryside and the mountains beyond, still snow-capped in the height of summer. He knew that from the other side of the palace could be seen Callier, Iondorra's capital city, almost Swiss in its cleanliness and gleaming, ordered precision. For a country that was primarily agricultural, Theo had been surprised to discover just how much the royal family had focused their energies on generating a strong capital, insisting on the development of a university to keep the next generation's interest, rather than seeing them look elsewhere for centres of learning and jobs.

He had done his research on Sofia long before their engagement—his private investigator having been working overtime for the past year in order to set this up. He'd begun the moment that he'd realised he could not let go. He'd often questioned what it must have taken to smooth out the rough, wayward edges of the reckless, almost wild girl he had once known. And he wondered, not for the first time, whether she missed that part of herself. The very part that had drawn him to her like a moth to a flame. Sofia's freedom, her carefree fire, had been too much for a boy who could never have afforded it for himself.

Maria was sat, bent over something small

and silvery by the window seat at the opposite end of the room.

'What do you have there?' he asked, forcing himself to turn away from his thoughts.

She looked up and smiled, her dark hair falling in a cascade over one shoulder. 'It's a piece I created for the exhibition in a few days' time,' she replied, offering up the necklace that fell like a river of silver from her hands. 'You're... you're still coming?' she asked. The way she failed to contain the mixture of hope and hurt in her eyes reminded Theo that they really did need to have that talk.

'You are going to sign this?' Sebastian demanded from behind him.

Theo's attention was called back to Sebastian where he sat reading the prenuptial agreement.

'Theo, you cannot sign this.'

'Of course I can.'

'I mean, I expected a few subclauses from her, but really? Twenty million euros to be paid in the event of your infidelity, scandal, or... Is "tomfoolery" even a legal term?'

'I believe she is trying to put me off. But it won't work.'

'If you sign this, then you are a madman.'

'Perhaps. If I had any intention of actually going through with the wedding.'

Theo turned to find both Sebastian and his sister, Maria, staring up at him in confusion. He wished they could have seen what they looked like, frozen in a tableau of shock. He nearly laughed. He had momentarily forgotten that Maria was there too, but he knew that Sebastian would never have kept his charade from her.

'Theo, what are you doing?'

'I am doing what I had always intended to do,' he said, watching Sebastian with heavy-lidded eyes. 'I am going to ensure that Sofia knows what it feels like to wait. To stand there and wonder, and doubt. To feel the humiliation, to have it marked upon her indelibly. I want her to wait there in front of her wedding guests, her country, at the church alone. To realise that I am not there and that I am not coming. I want her to suffer the consequences of her actions, as my mother and I suffered.'

'So, you don't love her?' Maria's quiet voice cut through the silence of the room.

'I could never love that woman.' *Not again.*

'Have you really thought this through?' Sebastian enquired.

'Every day for ten years.'

'What happens afterwards?'

'I'll release a statement saying that I could not force her into a loveless marriage. The press will lap it up. I will be saving her from herself and a marriage that would have broken her. I'll come out a hero.'

'That is cynical, even for you, my friend.'

Cynical maybe, but necessary. It was time that Sofia de Loria learned that there were consequences to her actions.

It had been years since Sofia had seen the palace's ballroom draped in such finery and filled with so many people. Her father's deterioration had consigned much of her small family's lives to brief external visits, rarely allowing for the opening of the palace, for outward glances to turn inward upon them. Sofia thought that the last time the ballroom had looked like this might have been her fifteenth birthday, before she'd been sent to boarding school and met the man that had brought this down upon her.

This evening was costing the country money

it barely had, but lord knew, everyone loved a royal wedding. It was an investment—for the future of her country. She had to see it as such or she'd curl into a ball in her room and never come out.

She resisted the urge to soothe her brow where the beginnings of a tension headache the size of the San Andreas fault line was gathering. She hated the fact that Theo had blackmailed her, hated that there was no confidant, no friend that she could turn to. Her entire life since leaving that school had been about training, learning the tools that she would need to put the country first. She'd had no time for friends, for people her own age. The last friend she'd thought she had was... Theo. With him, she'd been utterly herself.

It could have been so different, she thought. She'd once dreamed of it being different. The same man, yes. But this? No.

However, part of the future she was securing for her country required children. That thought sent sparks of fire and ice across her skin and down her spine. They hadn't yet discussed that. But she'd made sure to put it into the prenuptial agreement. She could be just as sneaky as he.

She'd thought with some small pleasure at how shocked he might be to read the clause that required his contribution to IVF treatment. She had absolutely no intention of sharing her bed with him. And even as she'd had that thought, her inner voice cried *liar*. It brought to mind memories of their kiss…the way her body had sung, had clung to him as desire moved like wildfire through her veins, as her body and soul had yearned for more.

The sudden and shocking thoughts raised a painful blush to her overly heated cheeks, and, cutting off her thoughts, she glanced again at the clock, placing the practised smile on her features to satisfy the eager curiosity of various visiting dignitaries. Where the hell was Theo? Perhaps he *had* seen the clause in the agreement and had decided to punish her temerity.

But that thought was completely overridden by the sense of unease beginning to build. Her father was set to make a royal appearance for only a short allotted time. It was needed for publicity, to soothe potentially ruffled feathers on the Iondorran council for the inappropriateness of her chosen fiancé. Theo didn't need to know that at least two whole weeks had been spent in tense negotiations as she'd lied and cajoled her father's old cronies into accepting Theo. She had extolled his virtues, instead of parading his vices, argued the strength of a true love match, even as the lies had caught in her throat. Unconsciously she had repeated the same pleas she had once made to her father, ten years before as he had tried to extricate her from the boarding school.

She'd been surprised how readily they came to her lips, how easily the same fidelity, emotion, desperation had come to her aid. And the privy council had believed it in a way that her father never had.

And now, when she needed Theo by her side, he was keeping her waiting, keeping her father waiting. His medication was working for the moment, but she knew better than most how quickly that could change. Once again, she absentmindedly rubbed her forearm, feeling the phantom ache where the accident—as she thought of it now—had fractured the bone there and bruised the ribs beneath. From across the room her mother had caught the unconscious action, and she sent her a reassuring look.

When she finally saw Theo at the top of the

grand sixteenth-century staircase, her breath caught in her throat. In the back of her mind she was a little jealous—surely this was the princess's moment, to stand atop the staircase and be admired? But this was no fantasy, and Theo was certainly no prince. Yet admired? Yes. He was.

He stood in between Sebastian Rohan de Luen and a young woman so like him that she must have been his sister. Sofia caught the exiled duke's eye, his gaze held just the fraction of a moment, and she saw something more than speculation towards the woman who was to marry his friend...something foreboding.

Theo's powerful frame unfolded down the stairs into a jog, an *actual* jog, towards her. Sofia's head almost whipped around to search for the long-ago voice calling in her mind—*No running in the Grand Room, Sofia!*

He came towards her so fast, she had no time to react, the expression of joy across his features so shocking to her that she didn't prevent the hands that came to her cheeks and took her face in a warm caress as he placed his lips gently against hers. Instantly he enveloped her senses, the soft, earthy smell of him, the traces of electricity that sparkled beneath the pads of his fingertips against her skin, the heat of his lips and the way her body unconsciously rose to meet him...all gone as suddenly as it came.

'*Kardiá mou*, my tardiness in unforgivable,' he said against her mouth, loudly enough for all about her to hear. Sighs rose up about her from the women and indulgent smiles painted the faces of Iondorra's staunchest male dignitaries.

For a moment, the space of a heartbeat, Sofia had been fooled, had been transported back to a time when his kisses seemed to be her whole world. The way she wanted to sink into the pleasure, the comfort, the... Before her mind could finish the thought, she remembered. Remembered it all. The blackmail, the darkness behind his actions, the belief he held that she had set him up...and in a rash and defiant act, she nipped at his bottom lip with her teeth, quick and hard. He pulled back his head in surprise.

'Let me be the first to draw blood, then, Theo,' she hissed in a voice audible only to him.

'No, Sofia. You did that years ago,' he said

darkly, his deft tongue sweeping at the thin
trace of crimson on his lip, before a mask descended over his features and he turned to the
gathering in the ballroom with a broad smile.

As Iondorra's leading figures lined up to pass
on their congratulations to the happy couple
Sofia and Theo continued their quiet lines of
attack in under-the-breath sentences.

'I thought I was supposed to be the one who
was fashionably late,' she whispered.

'Fashion doesn't have to be gender specific.'

'Your ego is impossible.' Sofia broke off to
welcome the Minister of Trade and Industry.
'Eugene, lovely to see you.'

'Your Highness, felicitations.' She nodded
her acceptance. As her father's trusted advisor
trailed off and they waited for the next, Theo
took up their conversation.

'It has serviced me well over the years.'

'It's not the only thing that serviced you,' she
bit out darkly.

'Come, now, Sofia, jealousy doesn't suit you.'
Before she could respond, he pressed on. 'You
look ravishing as always,' he said, turning to
take her in fully.

'That's what happens when the dress you

wear to your engagement party is picked by the privy council after three rounds of rigorous polling.'

'You would have chosen something different?'

'Why?'

'I'd like to know what façade I'm going to get. At least if you had chosen your own it would allow me to draw some conclusion about you.'

'Why do you want to draw a conclusion about me? Surely I'm only here to increase your wine sales,' she hissed as she turned to meet the next guest. 'Lord Chancellor,' Sofia said as she extended a hand to meet the last and final man in the greeting line.

Introductions over and done, they both turned to face the large ballroom. As they stood side by side, it could have been forgiven to see them as the happy couple looking over their guests.

'Your governance is modelled on the British system.'

Sofia shrugged a nonchalant shoulder. 'It worked for them.'

Theo inclined his head in agreement.

Sofia drew a deep breath, reluctantly steeling herself. 'It's time to see the king.'

She felt rather than saw Theo sweep his gaze across the crowded room. 'He's talking to someone—let's have a drink.'

Sofia pressed down on her panic. Her father had been here for fifteen minutes already and she didn't know how long he'd be able to continue before an episode began.

'Theo, please.' Whether it was the tone in her voice, or the fact her small hand had reached out to his, punctuating the request with a slight trace of desperation, she didn't know, but a low lean of his head gave his agreement.

Her mother met their approach with something like the same relief that Sofia felt. The moment this was done, protocol was met, her mother and father could return to the privacy of their suites.

'Your Majesty,' Sofia called to her father, instantly checking his eyes for signs of clarity or confusion, ready to whisk Theo away should the latter be the case. Her father took in the sight of her, assessment shining in his eyes. It gave nothing else away.

'Mother,' she said, pressing a kiss to each of her delicate cheeks.

'Father, may I present Theo Tersi,' she said,

stepping slightly to the side, and suddenly over-whelmed with the fear that Theo would do or say something wrong.

'Your Majesty,' Theo said with a bow from his lean neck, drawing to his full height as each man assessed the other.

Her father cut her a glance, one that took her immediately back to ten years before. Anger, a slight trace of confusion, marred the older man's frowning brow. Sofia bit back a curse. They had waited too long.

'I told you,' he growled, 'that you could not...' He trailed off for just a moment, giving her the only opening she knew she'd get. She remem-bered those words, too, from that night all those years ago. Was that where her father was in his mind? She forced a smile to her face, hoping that if she and her mother could maintain the farce, they might just get through this.

'That I could not find a better man. I know, Papa.' Not waiting for any further act that might give away his deterioration, she pressed kisses to each of his cheeks. Surprise and brief hap-piness shone in her father's eyes, warming the cool place of sadness in her heart. 'He's perfect, Papa,' she said, turning to Theo, whose quick mind must have already picked up that something wasn't quite right. 'And makes me truly happy.' As she said the words, she felt the now familiar sting of tears pressing against her eyes.

She saw her mother squeeze her father's arm in a gesture both comforting and grounding.

'I'm glad that you found each other again. It's good. It's right,' he declared finally and the breath that had been held universally across the ballroom was exhaled by all the guests.

Theo bowed once again at the older man before they exchanged a strong handshake, Theo holding it for perhaps just a moment longer than required.

Released from duty, Sofia had turned, pulling Theo with her, when her father called her back.

She leaned towards her father to hear his whispered words.

'*En garde*, Sofia. *En garde.*'

She nodded, feeling his words more truthful than any she'd heard him speak in the last five years. For just a moment she felt that her father was back, with her, protecting her and caring for her. Until she heard his next whispered words.

'And watch out for the German parachutist. Do not speak to him!'

Without having to look at her mother, who was the only other person to hear the king's incoherent warning, she replied, 'I will, Papa. I will.'

Theo had imagined meeting Sofia's parents many times, under many different circumstances. Ten years ago, he had not thought for a second that she was a royal in disguise. Nothing of what she had told him about her family had indicated any such thing. As an only child, like him, she had spoken of finding ways to amuse herself, spending hours delving into imaginary worlds within books, or running through gardens and woods. He had picked through each and every one of her words since he'd discovered that she was a princess—but, as with all good lies, much of it must have been taken from some thread of the truth. But the exchange with her father was...not what he'd expected.

He hadn't missed the moment of panic shared by the two women, mother and daughter, at the way the king's words hadn't quite fitted the situation. And, though he hadn't heard the last exchange, Theo hadn't missed the raw vulnerability in Sofia's eyes when she had proclaimed her happiness and his perfection.

Were they worried that the older man would rile against his common birth? Was her father furious that she was to wed a commoner? Theo had met much discrimination over the years, for various different reasons. He knew what it looked like, felt like and tasted like. And the king? He was not happy.

But he'd said 'again'. He was glad they'd found each other *again*. Which seemed to indicate that he knew about their relationship in the past, which confused him. He'd been convinced that she had kept him her dirty little secret, but—

'Whisky? We will toast with champagne, but if you wanted...'

His dark look at her must have thrown her as her words trailed off. Her eyes were overly bright, her words just a little too quick. What was going on? A slight noise behind him drew his gaze to see the retreating figures of the king and queen, discreetly spirited away through a side exit. And once again anger whipped through him.

'Your father isn't sticking around for the toast, then?' he couldn't help but bite out. Couldn't help but be transported back to a time when all he'd wondered was why his own father hadn't stuck around. Couldn't help but remember the way his family had treated his mother and himself because of it. Heat and hurt scorched him in an instant.

'No. He couldn't.' Before the growl could escape his lips, she pressed on. 'He's been… working hard and is tired.'

He was used to reflecting that every single word from her mouth was a lie, but this was different. There was the ring of truth in what she said, but there was also a shimmer of falsehood there too or, if not, then evasion distracting him from his reflections on the past.

The toast was given to them by a man he'd never seen before, but was probably a whole lot more appropriate than what Sebastian might have said to a room full of royals. He felt Maria's gaze on him throughout the evening, and not for the first time wondered whether if it might have been better to have let her believe the falsehood he was weaving through the night. She was young and impressionable and wholly overprotected by her brother.

Within an hour Theo was surprised to find himself on the verge of exhaustion. As a successful businessman and vintner, he was used to heading up million-dollar business meetings, but this constant diplomacy was tiring, yet Sofia showed no signs of fatigue, her fake smile—for he knew it to be fake—was undimmed and as fresh as the first one she had offered.

'Little Sofia,' said an older man with shocking white hair and a broad purple sash spotted with medals and pins that proclaimed his importance. He felt Sofia bristle beside him at the patronising appellation. Unconsciously his protective instincts rose, and he drew to his full height.

'Theo Tersi,' he said, stretching out his hand to sever whatever connection had sprung between his fiancé and the older man.

'Georges de Fontagne.'

'Monsieur de Fontagne is the Minister of Agriculture,' Sofia said, apparently finally finding her voice.

'Sofia,' greeted the small, birdlike woman

standing beside Georges, her diminutive stature only serving to magnify her husband's largess.

'Louisa,' Sofia replied with much more warmth.

When Louisa turned her smiling attention to him, Theo took her hand in his and raised it to his lips in such an old-fashioned move, he nearly surprised himself, satisfied to see that a small blush had risen to the older woman's cheeks as she smiled coyly.

'I wanted to offer my congratulations and beg that you satisfy my curiosity once and for all,' interrupted Georges. 'Please, do share the story of your rather *sudden* courtship.' His voice carried, as did the slight trace of cynicism heavy on his words. 'Do not tell me it was born of that horrifying trend of using matchmakers!'

The man's wife was looking thoroughly mortified at her husband's behaviour and Sofia, for the first time that evening, seemed shocked into silence. It was clear that the man knew something of Sofia's search in Paris six weeks before and was taunting her with it. It was untenable.

Theo might not have been born to this strata of society, but he knew in an instant that he had more manners in his little finger than this man did. It reminded him of the way that his mother's family had treated them, *before* he had turned the little dirt pile he and his mother had bought from her family into an award-winning vineyard. Before he had made enough money to buy out the remaining land his mother's family owned and shuffled them off to some distant part of Greece, only to be pulled out of their exile when he felt like it. Only his *giagiá* had taken pity on them, supported them through that first year and then afterwards when his mother became sick. Theo refused to acknowledge the perverse fact that he felt more than justified in seeking his own revenge, but would not counter an attack against Sofia from another quarter. And as such, all temptation to leave Sofia to stew in a mess of his making disappeared.

'We—' she started, but he squeezed her arm gently to stop her.

'*Agápi mou*, I have heard you tell this story before and your natural instinct towards modesty never does me justice. Allow me?' He watched her eyes widen just a fraction with surprise, and she nodded.

'I am sure that you will have heard something of my slightly *scandalous* reputation,' Theo confided ruefully to the couple. 'And I could not lie and say it is not deserved, as I had never thought to find a woman who could live up to the high standard set by my mother.'

From the corner of his eye, he saw Sofia struggle not to roll her eyes, and Louisa struggle not to sigh contentedly. His charm might not have been broadcast in the press, but it was no less potent a skill than his wine-making abilities and he was determined to use it now to its fullest.

'You see, years ago, when I was a young man, I fell deeply in love. I would have given everything for her, and in some ways did.' He felt Sofia flinch and could have sworn he heard the beat of her heart pick up in confusion as to where he was taking this fabricated story. 'But sadly it was not to be. So I hardened my heart, sure that I would never feel the same way again. And I was right.' He had predicted Louisa's brief gasp of shock, and had not been wrong as he'd imagined Georges' avaricious gaze ready for his next words. 'For when I met Sofia I realised that what I had thought was love was just a pale imitation.' Louisa melted, Georges scowled, and Sofia...he simply couldn't tell.

'From the first moment that I laid eyes on her I knew I was completely ruined...' He paused to see if even this would bring Sofia out of her perfect façade, and, though she paled just slightly, no outward sign of upset showed. 'Ruined for other women for ever,' he concluded. 'I knew that she was the woman that I wanted to spend the rest of my life with. You may dismiss that as pure fantasy. Or something based purely on her beauty. But it wasn't. Every word, movement, decision, enthralled. Her intelligence, her poise and, just as much, her playfulness. Did you know that Sofia has a naughty streak?'

'I remember as much from her childhood,' Georges said critically.

'Ah, but this is what makes Sofia so perfect, for while a country needs an iron-willed ruler, the people need fun and authenticity. And that is what really drew me to Sofia. This I knew in just a moment, but Sofia needed a little more time than I. Oh, she made me work for it, I assure you, Georges,' he said, leaning towards the obese man to intimate confidence, while his skin crawled. 'Over our first lunch together, I produced my finest wine…knowing that I had to seduce her senses as much as her mind and heart. It was a very special bottle of wine for me. There were only three made, from the very first grape of my vineyard in the Peloponnese. The first was for my mother, my child will have the third, but Sofia…she had the second.

'Unbeknownst to me, in the years before we had met, I had created the perfect blend of wine, solely in preparation for her. The playful notes of blueberry and bay leaves grounded in the rich, deep Greek soil were simply…*her.*'

Theo realised, as he had spoken, he had caught her gaze with his, the words casting a spell that had drawn the attention not just of the horrible Georges and his poor wife, but also that of the surrounding courtiers and dignitaries. A pin dropped to the floor could have been heard in the silence.

Sofia's face was upturned to his, only a few inches between them, shock and surprise evident in her eyes. He felt, as much as saw, her draw a deep breath, stealing the air from before him. In the silence everything disappeared. The room, the guests, the past…and he was seventeen all over again, looking at the young Sofia as her unpractised body begged him to take her lips. Need and desire encased them, separating them from the rest of the world. The stark sensuality of her calling to him across the years, the months, days and seconds.

He dipped his head, closing the distance between them, and drank from her lips, tasting all the flavours he had just described. The slight sting from where she had indelicately bitten him earlier making it so much more sweet.

Then she opened for him and he plunged into the soft warmth of her mouth, teasing them both with swift movements of his tongue, delving deep within her and relishing every moment.

The roaring in his ears shifted and morphed into the sound of a hundred hands clapping, and just as many voices cheering. He pulled back, suddenly shocked by his own actions mirrored in Sofia's gaze and kiss-bruised lips.

CHAPTER FIVE

'WHAT ON EARTH were you thinking?' Sofia demanded the moment she collected herself after *that kiss*, and the moment they were free of Georges and Louisa's attention.

'I was thinking that it would be the only thing that might wipe the insidious smirk from that obnoxious man's face.'

'You think *he* is obnoxious? Really?'

'I do.'

'He is an important man in the ministerial cabinet, Theo, I cannot afford—'

'The girl I once knew didn't give a flying fig for what she could or could not afford, Sofia. Tell me, where has she gone?' he asked, searching her face, 'for I cannot find a trace of her anywhere.'

'People change,' Sofia replied, turning away from his penetrating stare. Everyone changed. Her father, Theo, herself. No one was who they once were.

But not everything changed, her inner voice taunted her.

No. The way he had kissed her hadn't changed. The moment his lips had pressed against hers, first in that momentary initial greeting, and then later with *that kiss*, it had felt like…home. Some imaginary place in her mind when it had just been the two of them, all those years ago, with no concerns other than how soon they could see each other again. His body had called to hers in the same way it had done all those years ago, and she hated him for it. Because he was right. That girl was gone and she could never come back. Not if she wanted to secure a future for her country. They needed the royal woman she had become, regal and poised. So she delved into the inner strength she had forged from the loss of her hopes and dreams and became that woman again.

She barely spared Theo another glance as she visited with dignitaries, accepted their congrat-ulations, agreed to visit with various countries after the wedding—and if her heart stuttered over that precise word or moment to come, then she ignored it as she made plans for a future she could no longer see.

Despite her attempts to relegate Theo to the sidelines, he hovered almost constantly by her side, dishing out the same charm he had drowned Louisa de Fontagne in, showing a peculiar adroitness in conversation with the various ministers and members of the privy council. And slowly she began to form an image of the man to replace that of the boy she had known. One who had skilfully nurtured an international wine conglomerate from a small part of Greece, one who seemed to have lost some of that inner sense of insecurity she had once recognised as being similar to her own, a sense of not quite being rich enough, or good enough...

'I must say, I'm impressed,' he said into the air just above her head. For all the world they would look like a couple very much in love as she tilted her face towards his. Only he could read the confusion in her eyes. 'One could be forgiven for thinking that this was an engagement party rather than an opportunity for you to network. But so far I have seen you organise at least three potential trade agreements with all the panache of a seasoned CEO.'

'Don't think I didn't miss the mention of

your precious wine whilst you were talking to Georges. He was practically begging you for shares in your company once he realised that his wife, along with half the world, would seek out the magical wine blend that tasted *just like me*. It was a nice touch, by the way.'

'It was, wasn't it?' The pleasure was evident in his voice. 'You'll have to add it to the cover story your council made so hastily. Really, Sofia? You thought that the world would believe we had been introduced by a mutual friend? That's akin to saying we met on Tinder. But, as you know well, the best lies always have a hint of the truth.'

He waited until he had caught her gaze once more. 'Why did you not tell them we had met at school? Worried they would dig up my expulsion?' He wanted to look in her eyes as she answered his question. Wanted to see the truth she had somehow been able to hide from him. 'Or were you just worried about the world's press uncovering my low upbringing?'

'I never thought that of you, Theo. You were the only one who did,' she said in softly spoken words, and it was not an accusation, but he felt it as such.

Theo scoffed. 'You really have no idea, do you?' It took nothing to bring to mind a childhood that had felt like death by a thousand cuts, a thousand stares, snide comments and a fair few beatings when his mother wasn't looking. 'Up there, the little princess in the ivory tower.' He jerked his head up through the floors above the grand ballroom towards an unseen turret. 'Did you really not see the stares, or hear the words whispered by teachers and students alike? Do you really not know how the world *works*, Sofia? How the powerful turn on the weak in any attempt to guard their pedestal of superior wealth or position? Is it an accident of your birth, or wilful ignorance? I honestly can't tell any more. Because you were, are, many things, Sofia, but I didn't think that naïve was one of them.'

Her eyes turned the dark blue of an electrical storm. 'Naïve? You know nothing of what I have sacrificed—'

'What have you ever sacrificed, Sofia?'

You, the thought screamed silently in her mind. Anger rode her pulse to impossible speeds, her chest heaving against the low cut of her dress. An anger so much like desire—

the fire in her blood quick to make the leap from one to the other. She felt the breadth of his shoulders expand beside her, and the way he stood proprietorially seemed to encase her, preventing her from seeing beyond the wall of the toned muscles of his chest, cutting her off from the room beyond. It was too much, the closeness of their bodies, the heat pulsating between them, the way her own body seemed to lean towards him as if wanting to pull rather than push him away.

'I didn't think so,' Theo said in the space of her silence. 'I look around the room, this party, this palace and see numbers. Because after I returned to Greece with my mother, it was all about numbers. The number of universities that retracted their scholarship offers after my expulsion. The number of family members that turned their backs on us, the single digit representing the one person willing to help. The number of euros begged and borrowed to buy that first plot of land, the number of times my mother and I went without food, the number of sleepless nights that wrecked us both as we plunged everything we had into that first grape harvest. The number of bottles we were first able to sell, after the number of failed attempts that preceded it. But do you know what doesn't have a number? How *hard* it was.'

She watched him with large, round eyes, and he imagined the pity there, surely. The way her eyes glinted with compassion just a remnant of what he wanted to see.

'I'm so sorry. Truly. I wish I could have helped.'

'Helped?' he demanded, the word almost getting stuck behind his outrage. 'I'm not talking about the work. I would do that every day for the rest of my life and still be happy. What was hard was the belief that *I* had done this to my mother. That *I* had brought this upon the one person in my life who had ever loved me. That, had I not fallen for your pretty lies, then I would have graduated at the top of my class, I would have attended one of the finest universities in the world with a scholarship. My future and my mother's would have not been filled with struggle and numbers of loss… I could have given her the world. For years I felt the weight of that on my shoulders. Until I realised that I was wrong. It wasn't my fault, it was yours. You laid a trail of pretty little lies like breadcrumbs for me to follow all the way to my destitution. And I believed those lies.

'How ironic that we survived the abandonment of my father, only to be cut down at the knees by a pampered princess. One that, no matter how exhausted I was, how many hours I worked in the dust, the mud, the earth, no matter how much I sweated, gained or lost... was the only thing I could think of each and every night. You.'

But his words had come out wrong. He felt the way they tasted on his tongue, heard the way they hit the air between them. He had meant it as a castigation, as an explanation or excuse for what he felt he had to do, all the things that Sofia didn't yet know of. But even to his own ears it had sounded more like a plea. A plea that he could not allow for, so he pressed on with the cruel taunt he knew would drive his desire for her away like no other.

'Until you married someone else.'

The last blow was too much for Sofia to bear. Each word, each statement filling in the blanks in her knowledge of him, changing and reforming what she had imagined for him in the years since that night ten years ago, had twisted the knife deeper in her breast. Until that final mention of Antoine. Her fingers reached for the comfort of the wedding band that was no longer there. Instead they scraped against the cold cut of the diamond that had been delivered to the palace two weeks before, the unfamiliar shape beneath the tips of her fingers cold and harsh. Another ring, worn from duty rather than desire or love.

She knew that she should tell him what had happened that night, knew that she should explain how she hadn't set him up to take the fall for her foolish actions, make him understand that she'd had no choice that night, or any since. Desperately she wanted to tell him that she had meant every word, every hope she'd ever shared with him, but what would it achieve? One part knew he'd not believe her and the other part knew she could not even if he might. The reason she had left that night was bound in secrecy and desperation, to protect her family from what was now only just around the corner. Did it really matter what he thought of her? Only to Sofia. It didn't change anything. Didn't change the fact she needed to be married, needed to no longer be the Widow Princess when the time came for her to assume the throne.

'I simply cannot fathom why you would have married a man who—'

'What, Theo? Wasn't you?' she demanded, cutting into his sentence before he could cause even more pain by maligning Antoine. 'For all this talk of vengeance and needing to teach me the consequences of my actions—yes, I *was* paying attention in Paris—what is it really? That I dared to marry another man? Is your ego really that significant to you?'

His head reared back as if he'd been slapped and the thin shred of satisfaction at the sight made her feel both jubilant and petty at the same time.

'What would make you feel better, Theo? To hear that I didn't love him? Well, I did. He was a good, kind man who understood me, understood what I needed. Who also understood what my position meant in a way that you *never* will. I am truly sorry that you've faced such hardships, Theo. I am sorry that you feel responsible for them, I am also sorry that you believe that I caused that, that I did that to you. But if that's what you need to do, then so be it.

'And if you need to hear that Antoine and I didn't have the chemistry you seem to effortlessly taunt me with, then fine. We didn't. Does it please you to know that he took lovers? That it shamed him as much as me? Would that help? Do you need to know that each and every touch left me cold and more alone than I can possibly describe? Because the only person whose touch I had ever craved was you? The only person I had ever imagined sharing that part of myself with, was you? Would that ease your ego?'

Shame and misery sobbed in her chest, and tears that had formed without her knowledge or permission gathered behind the lids of her eyes, casting both Theo and the room about them in a blurry haze. She couldn't stand it any more, couldn't stand here knowing that he had drawn from her a secret that she had shared with no other.

So she fled her engagement party, turning her back on the gathered guests, picking up the skirts of her dress as she almost ran from the ballroom.

* * *

There were very few times in his life that Theo could remember being shocked into silence, and each and every one of them involved Sofia. But none of them had hit him with the power of a tsunami. Waves of something he did not want to put a name to crashed against him as he followed in her wake. He didn't care if he drew the curious glances of strangers as he left the ballroom with determined steps. He didn't care if they would have to come up with yet another story to define or excuse their actions and their engagement.

All he cared about was what Sofia had revealed to him, and if it made him want to beat his chest with pride and need, and ego, then so be it, even if it made him a bastard. His pulse raged and he felt the burn in his thighs as he took several steps at once towards her suite, feelings that he relished as he ate up the distance she had tried to put between them.

She had told him many lies in the past, but what she had said about her first husband, what she had said about *him*? That was most definitely the truth, and had somehow worked to lift the self-imposed barrier he had placed between them. Now, though, *now* there was no turning back.

Even as he stalked the palace hallways towards her room he felt the rush of desire, the swelling of arousal in his groin, the thickening of this band of want and need around his chest and throat. It might not have changed his plans for her, no. He would still have his revenge. But perhaps if he gave in to this insane desire burning between them, then he might finally be able to rid himself of the devastating hold she had over him. No, not him. His libido. He was a man of flesh and blood, and he would not deny either of them a taste of their basest desires.

He flexed his hand as it trembled ever so slightly in the space between him and the door to her rooms, and thrust it back by his side. Instead, he pushed the door open and kicked it shut behind him as he stepped over the threshold and drank in the sight of his prey.

She sat at the dressing table, staring off into the distance, looking as alone and isolated as she had claimed to be only moments earlier. Her golden hair, swept back into a chignon, glistened in the dimly lit room, matched only by the sparkle of the diamonds around her neck, dipping towards the V in her chest, and he stood half mesmerised by the sight of the rise and fall of her breasts, the only outward sign of her distress...

For the first time in years he felt an affinity with her, as he recognised that they were both in thrall to the spell of desire wrapping around them in great swathes of need.

'Stop.'

'Stop what?'

'This,' she said, gesturing between them. 'Whatever it is you're doing, just stop.'

'I would if I could, Princess, trust me.'

'You don't even like me,' she said, unable to help the smallness of her voice.

'I don't have to like you to want you,' he growled, the admittance rough on his voice. 'It's as if it's ingrained in me as much as my childhood lessons. When I should have been learning algebra, instead I learned the cosine of your skin, the angle of your chin, the circumference of your waist and the weight and feel of your breast. When I should have been learning French, instead I learned the language of the sighs of your pleasure, the rhythm and cadence of your pulse and your desire—'

'Stop,' she tried again, but failing to hide the pleading tone in her voice. And that plea called to him, taunting him, challenging him.

'No, Sofia. Because while I learned all these things, you seemed only to learn self-denial and how to lie.'

'And you are here to teach me my own body, Theo?' she asked, incredulity clear in her oceanic eyes.

He couldn't help the bitter laugh that left his lips. 'I would teach you how to demand the pleasure you so desperately plead for, beneath your cultured, perfect words. To unearth the truth of what your body craves beneath your mind's barriers. *Theé mou*, the Sofia I knew would have not hesitated.'

'I don't have to like you to want you.'

The words echoed in her mind. No, 'like' was too easy a word for what lay between them. He blamed her for every awful thing that had happened to him since that night ten years ago, and she blamed him for blackmailing her into this farce, for stealing her choice, even as he professed to give her a choice over this.

'I don't have to like you to want you.'

As if that one true acknowledgement had the power to unlock the cage she had just placed her inner self, her desires and wants into, need escaped as if his voice, his words were the key, twisting again and again within a lock so secure she had thought it never to be opened again.

'You want me?' Sofia said, with a voice raw with desire, turning to stand from the chair and stepping towards him. 'Take me,' she demanded.

He shook his head. Slowly. Not once taking his eyes from hers. 'Oh, no, Sofia. You're going to have to do better than that. You will not be passive in this, I won't allow you to hide behind excuses, proclaiming that I drove you to this. No. If *you* want *me*...then take *me.*'

The spell that had bound her from her wants and needs lifted, the challenge he laid at her feet rose into her accepting hands. Hands that tingled with the need to feel his bare skin beneath them.

Could she? Could she really do this? His words were a call to action, but her insecurities held her back. She wanted this. Wanted him with a need that shocked her, scared her even.

But she had never done this before, certainly not with her husband… In truth she'd always dreamed of what it would be like with Theo. Fevered dreams, ones that had left her heated and wanting and unfulfilled.

She crossed the distance between them in shaking strides and when she stood before him, a hair's breadth between them, it was as if she didn't know where to start. She wanted it all. Years of hunger made her body stronger than her indecision. Her fingers trembled as they reached just beneath his perfect suit jacket to slip it from his shoulders, and leave it discarded by their feet.

They were on fire as they went to the silk tie around his neck and fed it through the loop that held it secure. She slid it from the collar of his shirt, focusing on the top button and fumbling slightly.

'Look at me,' he commanded. But she wasn't ready yet. She wasn't ready for him to see the desire and need and…innocence she felt shining from her skin, let alone her eyes. She wasn't ready for him to see the truth of her need for him, because if he did he would know. Know that she hadn't the faintest idea of what she was doing.

She slipped the button through its moorings, her thumb tracing a small pathway over hair-roughened skin, the heat from the contact spreading across the back of her hand, up her elbow and straight to her chest. Another button undone, and another tantalising glimpse of the hard planes of his chest...her hands awkward as they lifted the shirt tails from within the belt of his trousers.

Her fingers slid beneath the white cotton onto his deeply tanned abdomen, rippling beneath her touch, causing her to wonder at the evidence of the effect of her caress. His chin nudged her head to the side as he sought access to her neck. But she pulled away from the reach of his lips. He had told her to take him. So she would.

Unconsciously she arched against his chest like a cat, and when he nudged her thighs apart with his own she nearly cried out loud. The thick muscled thigh rubbing the soft silks of her skirt between her own legs was driving her senses wild. The low thrum that had started at her core now roared to life, pulsing with need for satiation, for his touch, for him.

She pushed him back against the wall, relishing her power, never having guessed that she would feel such a thing in this moment. Their bodies collided as his back pressed against the wall, her breasts aching for him.

She slid the shirt from his shoulders, broad and powerful from hard work and intense labour, and her hands swept behind him as he leant forward, allowing her nails to scratch at the thick, corded muscles, bunched with tension. His head rocked back as she did, a growl on his lips she desperately wanted to silence, because it heightened her own need and pleasure.

A pleasure she sought desperately from him as she learnt the adult body of a boy she had once desired, whilst punishing him by withholding a kiss...because if they kissed she might never find her way back. Instead of seeking his lips, she pressed hers against the suntanned skin of his chest, finding the spot beneath his ribs that caused him to suck in a lungful of air.

His hand came round to grasp her hip, and

she brushed it away, refusing to let him share this moment of power she had only just discovered for herself. Within herself. The power that somehow he had given her to finally take what she'd wanted for so, so long.

Her tongue found his hard, flat nipple and flicked, the slight bucking of his body speaking only to the leash of control he was holding so strongly. She hated it, hated that he might have control over something that was almost totally overwhelming her.

Her hands went to his belt and drew the leather apart with a snap. The *hiss* as she undid the zip on his trousers was the only sound other than that of their pleasure, loud in the room.

His hands bunched the silk of her skirt at her thighs, pressing it against her skin as he drew the material higher and higher. Her hand went to his wrist, halting his progress, and a battle of wills ensued, finally drawing her eyes to him. He waited, tension evident in the dark blush against his exquisite cheekbones…waited for her permission to continue, and she marvelled at it. This game of power that was unspoken but clear in every movement, every sigh, every touch.

She released the hold she had on his wrist, and he lifted the skirts of her dress to her waist, one hand pinning the material, the other, pressed between her legs, paused, waiting, allowing the heat from his hand to soothe the ache caused by sheer need.

Sofia couldn't help a blush of embarrassment, as the evidence her desire had dampened the silken thong, and her body rippled as his thumb slid beneath the thin barrier to find her, wet and wanting.

Her head was flung back as the pad of his thumb found her clitoris and he stroked and stroked, ringing a pleasure so acute her legs began to shake. She had no idea that it could be like this, that somehow she had *denied* herself this all these years. She shifted as his hand turned, as his finger plunged into her, the strong, thick cords of his forearm almost holding her in place, holding her where he wanted and where she needed.

'Look at me,' he commanded, and this time she was unable to refuse. The deep brown of his eyes were drowned in pupils so large with desire she lost herself in the dark depths of them.

His lips crashed down upon hers, his tongue

prying them open and plunging into her mouth as if he needed to consume her whole. As his tongue delved, so did his fingers, deeper and harder, bringing her to a point she didn't yet want to reach.

Her hands flew back to his trousers, pressing gently at the hard ridge of his arousal, even while her inner sense reeled in shock at her actions, and this time she felt the growl building in the back of his throat. Her fingers reached beneath the waistband of his underwear, desperate for the hot, silken skin covering a steel-like need. A string of Greek curses, too quick for her to decipher, littered the air.

'Bed,' he demanded against her lips.

'No.'

He prised open his eyes to take her in, the fierce look of need and want calling to him in a way he had never imagined, her eyes a shimmering turquoise he had never seen before.

'I need to be very clear on what you are saying no to, Sofia,' he said with a growl.

'The bed, I'm saying no to the bed.'

She glanced at it as if fearful…and perhaps it was not the bed itself but the intimacy it invited. And, while they might be tearing clothes instead of strips off each other, perhaps for her that kind of intimacy between them was not welcome.

'If there is anything else you need to say no to...' He had been called a lot of names in his life, some of which he'd earned, but one thing he would never do was force a woman against her will. There was a special circle in hell reserved for men like that.

He held his breath. It would be hard, but if she asked, he would walk away. Walk away and not look back. He watched as his tone settled about her and she realised the truth of his words.

'I'm saying yes, Theo.'

'You always were contrary,' he growled as he crushed his lips against hers, knowing that there would be no going back. No walking away. Not yet.

CHAPTER SIX

HE TOOK CONTROL as easily as she had given it away.

Peeling his back from the wall and walking her in his arms backwards towards the day-bed, he spun them round and pulled her down with him as he lay back on the large expanse of what was probably an original Louis XVI chaise longue.

She still wore her dress, and he his trousers, but frankly he didn't care. The entire length of her body was pressed against his, and it welcomed the light pressure with a sigh.

He had meant what he said. He didn't have to like her to want her. But maybe, he prayed, if they finally gave in to the power of the sensuality that held them together, it would be over. It would sever its hold. Because no matter what woman had graced his bed until now, it had always been her. Sofia. It was she who had called to him in his most fevered of dreams. But the soft-as-silk skin beneath his touch, the heated flesh that seemed to warm even the coldest depths of him, was not a dream, nor a fantasy. She was here. In his arms. And he couldn't get enough.

He drew a knee upward to secure her, imprison her between his legs. The long length of his thigh encased her hip, and she pressed her hands down onto the seat beneath them, holding herself up on toned arms that were deceptively strong.

He didn't want her above him, he didn't like the way she looked down upon him, but the slender neck exposed by the upsweep of her hair called to him. He could resist no longer. His lips and teeth gently nipped at the exposed sweet flesh there, and he inhaled, deeply drinking her in, the soft blueberry and bay scent, heated by her skin, almost a mirror of the first wine he had produced. *Theos*, had he been consumed by her even then? The story he had woven for the obtuse minister came back to haunt him, as did his proclamation that the greatest lies held a kernel of truth.

But he didn't want to think of the past, nor the future, he only wanted to think of now. Her sigh brought him back to the present as easily as if she were a witch who had summoned him.

She placed a hand on his chest, his heart leaping there beneath it, as if it had finally found a missing piece of itself, and he itched to bat it away. Instead, he took her hand in his and pressed his lips against her palm, and even as his body cried out for quick release from this sensual prison he forced himself to stop and savour her as he would a wine. Surely only when he had identified each of the individual flavours, notes of what was unique to her, he would be satisfied, he would *know*.

He took each of her fingers, one by one, into his mouth, his tongue gently sucking on them, relishing the different sounds that fell from her lips as he did so. With one hand he traced the line of her delicate wrist, up to the elbow joint, around the firm muscles beneath her shoulder, and back up to her neck.

She rubbed against him, cradled in his hips, drawing an arousal so acute, so swift, it was almost painful. Once again the game of power was being played between them as she moved to take what she wanted.

He pulled her into his arms, and turned them

so that her back was now against the chaise longue, and he was above her, surrounding her with his shoulders and body, and she knew it from the look that entered her heated aquamarine gaze. There was too much assessment there, too much calculation. He wanted her blind with pleasure, as blind as he was at risk of becoming.

He took her lips with his, pressing against the perfect pink plumpness, lathing it with his tongue, drawing moans of pleasure as he plunged into her hot, wet depths, knowing that they were both imagining his tongue somewhere else on her body.

He wanted skin against skin, he wanted to see the rosy, taut nipple he could feel pressing through the material that separated them. He wanted to taste it, tease it.

The dress was beautiful, but it was in the way. His hands ran down her sides, looking for a zip, something, anything to release her from the wrapping and get to the present of her body beneath. He groaned when he could not find anything.

'Theo?'

'The dress…it's…'

She groaned her own frustration. 'It needed nearly two people to get me into the damn thing.'

He looked down on her, for a moment their shared frustration a shared amusement.

'It will only need me to get you out of it,' he said, giving her one last assessing gaze before he took the bottom of the dress, found the side-seam and tore apart the fabric with his hands.

The squeal, almost guilty in its pleasure, that came from Sofia drew an impossible smile from his lips. A smile that died the moment he took in the body that he had been dying to see, touch, taste for nearly ten years.

She was incredible. Her chest bare to him completely, the perfect rounds of her breasts, full and almost tear-shaped against her torso, only her modesty covered by the thin scrap of lace that he had encountered between her legs. She tried to hide from him, her face turned aside as if she was embarrassed by her own skin. Her knees came together before him, as if she was protecting herself from him. He couldn't help the words of praise that fell against her skin.

'Do not hide from me, Sofia. Not now,' he

growled, hating how his voice almost broke under the power of his arousal, of his desire for her. His hands went to her knees, gently levering them apart to make room for him as he leaned over her, finally taking one of her nipples between his lips, lathing it and toying it into perfect hard submission.

Her back arched upwards, against his mouth, the almost sob that fell from her lips the greatest satisfaction. He worked his mouth and lips lower, in open-mouthed kisses, leaving a damp trail that he knew the air would cool, sending shivers of arousal over her skin.

'Theo,' she begged and the sound of his name on her pleasure-filled voice nearly undid him.

'You want me here, Sofia? My touch, my tongue?' he demanded.

'You would make me beg?' Her voice broke.

'I would make you own it, own your pleasure, Sofia.'

Each time he said her name, her pupils dilated with pleasure. He almost couldn't say it enough. She nodded but it wasn't enough. He wanted to hear it, hear her wants, desires... *needs*.

For a moment they simply stared, the war of

control ebbing and flowing between them like a tide, as he held himself back from what they both so desperately wanted. Until she said it, until she commanded it, until she gave in to it.

'Yes, Theo. I want—'

Her words were lost to a cry of pleasure as he pulled aside the thin, silken material between her legs, as he uncovered the heart of her with his tongue, as he lathed the length of her and returned again and again to the one place that drew the most exquisite sounds of tormented need from her.

Her hips bucked beneath his ministrations, and he placed a hand low on her abdomen to hold her in place for him, his thumb stroking the silken curls hiding her womanhood.

He took her to the brink of her pleasure again and again, refusing to let her fall. Because when she did, he wanted her to be there with him.

'Theo, please...'

He knew what she wanted, what *he* wanted, for the first time their needs the same.

He reached into the pocket of the trousers he still wore, finding the slim wallet and retrieving the foil packet it contained. He left her body only to discard the trousers, never once taking his eyes from her, as he placed the latex over himself.

'This is the last time I will ask, Sofia. If you have any doubts—'

This time it was she that cut off his words, reaching up to pull him down to her, her hot hand like an anchor at the base of his neck, her legs parting for him as if welcoming him home, her lips barely an inch away from his as she said, 'This is what I want, Theo. That is the last time you will ask me.'

Never had he seen her so regal, so commanding, so powerful in her focus, her intent, her need.

He slid into her, filling her slowly, shifting and…

And the moment he felt her tense, he stopped. Shock and surprise as much in him as it was in her. *Theos*, he hadn't even thought. Hadn't even imagined…

'Sofia—'

'Wait, please…just…'

His body was almost shaking, and he bit back the curse that lay on his tongue. As the implications of her innocence struck him, anger poured through him and he realised the true extent of the lies of her first marriage. She was a virgin and he had not known. And somewhere deep within him that made him both fiercely angry and deeply satisfied. But he held back, because he knew his fury would scare her. *Damn*, her naivety burned him, etching her name on his soul.

As her body relaxed into him, she moved her hips experimentally beneath him.

'Sofia,' he tried again, tried to warn her of what she had already lost.

'I knew what I was asking for, Theo.'

No, she hadn't known. But she would. Soon, she would know and for the first time he hated himself for the path he had set for them both.

She shifted once more against him, his body utterly at her mercy now. All thought fled and, coward that he was, he hid in his body's needs, in Sofia's wants, and finally released the hold he had on his control.

Gently, so gently, he withdrew from her, only to resume a torturously slow return. Subconsciously his body recognised the difference, the change from hurried intent to languorous pleasure, pleasure that was to be all hers.

Theo lost track of time in the sounds of her

cries, needful and wanting, he knew only the ripple of her skin, the acres of smooth silk beneath his hands, the warm, luxuriously wet heat of her as he drew them towards the point of completion again and again.

Finally, at Sofia's desperate pleas, he took them into an abyss full of starlight and his last thought was that he was fundamentally changed for ever.

As the water poured over her skin, her heart still racing from what they had shared, still pounding before she'd even lifted her eyes to the scattered stars across the still night sky through the large windows of her room, she marvelled at the stretch of unfamiliar muscles across her body. Languid, but poised, as if already wanting Theo again.

She had meant what she'd said. She *had* known what she was asking for, asking of him. But she had not realised that it would make her feel… She shook her head in the shower, scattering drops of water from her hair. What did she feel? It was too much for words.

But there were words she did know. She knew that they needed to talk. Needed to confront the past…or as much of that night, ten years before, as she would be able to share. Because whether he'd wanted to or not, he *had* given her a moment of choice, of control. And as a result, it had become vital that she explain, vital that he knew that she hadn't had a choice when she'd left that night. That she hadn't purposefully set him up as he clearly believed. She couldn't tell him everything, the secret that locked her heart tight against the truth of her father's diagnosis, the secret that was to protect her country from instability and chaos, one so deep she wasn't sure she'd ever be able to reveal it. But she hoped that she could give him something… give him some sense of resolution about the past. Give him some truth amongst the one lie she still maintained.

She left the shower, wrapping herself in the large towel and retrieving a lightweight trouser suit, readily accepting any armour she could against the conversation that she knew would follow, any protection against Theo's impossibly penetrating gaze.

She dressed and went to sit beside the large windows, peering through the darkness to the elusive shadowscape of her beautiful country.

The rolling hills she knew lay beneath the deep night, the mountains in the distance, and all the sleeping inhabitants of Iondorra in between. She heard him stir behind her, the sound of his roughened palm against the smooth silk of the chaise longue, consciously or unconsciously reaching for her, she wondered.

'We should talk.'

'Then I should have coffee.'

She gestured to a coffee machine in the corner of the living suite of her rooms. Soon, she heard the spluttering, juddering sound it made as it filled the air with the fragrant, almost bitter taste of coffee that instantly made her mouth water, and turned to find him standing there in his suit trousers and nothing else. She pushed down the distraction of the smooth planes of sun-darkened skin across his powerful torso. They needed to have this conversation. If there was any hope...

'If we're going to marry—'

'If?'

'*If* we're going to marry, then we need to clear the air. We... I need to tell you about that night.'

Nothing in him moved, not a muscle or a flicker of his eyes. Brooding and powerful.

She'd always sensed that ability in him, latent, shimmering beneath the surface, but now? Now it had exploded in a technicolour aura that even the most obtuse would be able to identify. The alpha.

'Would you like to sit?' she said, gesturing to one of the two chairs framing yet another large set of windows.

'I'll stand.'

She nodded, returning her gaze to the panes of glass, but instead only seeing his reflection appearing behind her. Somehow she had always felt his presence, waiting, hovering over her shoulder.

'It may not surprise you to know that I was a wilful child. Stubborn and mischievous. My parents despaired of me. I managed to outwit at least three of the most professional nannies and au pairs Europe had to offer. Two were more than happy to sign non-disclosure agreements protecting their reputations as much as my family's. The last, instead, chose a change in her career path. I believe she is now working with horses.' She paused, taking a breath. Steeling herself against what she was to say. 'It's hard to explain what life was like growing up the only child to two parents whose first and last duty is to their country. Especially when one's own nature seems to run contrary to that sense of duty and self-sacrifice.

'When my parents agreed to enter me at the boarding school with my mother's maiden name, it was excused as being for my protection,' she said, with an absent laugh. 'It may have even been to protect the royal name, in case my wildness ruined that too.'

'In case?' Theo queried, as if the thought of her being anything other than the reckless, wayward teenager was impossible.

'But for me it was my *one* chance. Not to be seen as a royal, not to be the woman who would one day rule a country from beneath her father's long shadow, he the perfect king, and me the improper princess. In truth, we're quite minor royals in the grand scheme of Europe's nobility. It was surprisingly easy, especially given the infamy of many of the other students at the school.

'And at first it *was* easy. Creating the lies that kept my identity secret. They gave me protection from having to join many of the friendship groups my parents thought would help iron out my unsuitable behaviours. It allowed for me to be seen as *me*. And you were such a breath of fresh air to me, and I… I relished it. You didn't treat me as if I would break, or as if I was a disappointment, a failure. You just saw…me. You laughed with me, teased me and I couldn't get enough.

'Rather than bowing and bending to the rules of the school, I struggled against them, seeing it only as another form of constraint, another cage I would eventually swap with a crown.' Sofia took a deep sigh, sore and hurting for the child she had been. 'Much of my behaviour then was selfish and, yes, without thought for the consequences of my actions. I am sorry that I lied to you about who I was but… at the time it was my only comfort. The only light I felt within a bound and trapped existence.'

She watched as Theo shook his head against her words. 'You may excuse your lies as much as you want, but you knew what you were doing, *knew* that it was impossible for you to run away with me as you begged me to.'

She shrugged her shoulders helplessly. 'I think… I think that I believed the story I had told. I wanted so much to go with you, to run away from the school, from my responsibilities, from my future. The hours we spent talking about how it would be, where we would go, they had painted a future so firm in my mind that I...' She had thought she would die if she did not live it. 'Honestly, Theo—of all things, believe that what we shared was what was in my heart. I had no intention of making you take the fall for the prank on the headmaster's car. I had no intention of you being expelled.'

'Then what happened?' he demanded.

'I'd been furious with the headmaster. In design class, I and three others had been assigned a group project, but Anna—one of the group—had needed to return home and failed to pass on her part of the project and the remaining three of us were given detentions by the headmaster for not fulfilling the brief. It seems so petty now, but...then? It had seemed like a great injustice. So we hatched the prank to end all pranks. He loved his Mini Cooper. It was the most precious thing he owned, I think. We realised that if we could put two long planks up against the side of the sports hall, we could get the car onto the roof. Between us, the weight of the car wasn't too much, but the sharp edge of the wheel arch hurt, so I used your scarf to protect my hands and… I must have left it behind.

'I had arranged to meet you, to tell you about it. That was my surprise. I had…been showing off, I suppose. But an hour before I was supposed to meet you that night, there was a knock at my door. When I saw my parents standing there, I thought that they had discovered my part of the prank, I thought that they might have discovered my relationship with you. I was frightened then. For you, for me… So I was confused when…'

And now she began to pick and choose her words. She couldn't reveal her father's diagnosis. They were not yet married, the risk to the country still too great. Perhaps if somehow they managed to pull this marriage off then she could finally unburden herself of her secrets. But not yet. She had already prepared this speech, spent hours of each night in the last month, since he'd forced her hand, trying to work out the best possible threads to share, to unearth, to expose…

'They told me they had come to take me home. Iondorra was in a delicate state politically. There was a trend at the time for the smaller European countries to exchange royal rule for political governance, but our parliament was neither old nor strong enough to assume control. But there was enough talk within the parliament to force my father's hand and have me return in order to assume responsibilities much sooner than intended.'

He had still not moved, and she was still ensnared in his predatory gaze, as if his eyes were gently pressing against her words to find the truth of them.

'That night it was agreed that I would return to the palace, and begin learning what I would need.'

She had thought that at the very least she'd have two years before she would even have to start thinking of assuming royal duties. Two years in which maybe she could come to an understanding with her father...and if her father could just *meet* Theo—see what she saw in him—maybe she could somehow get him to recognise their marriage. Even now, her thoughts showed just how naïve she had truly been then.

In a rush she had told her parents about him. Explained that she was in love, begged and pleaded with them not to do this. Not to take her away from him. She remembered the way she had pulled on her father's lapels with white-knuckled hands, the way her mother had looked at her with both sympathy and pity.

But, as had been made painstakingly clear to her that night, she was their country's future and could no longer entertain a dalliance with 'that Greek', as her father had called him, her father's fear and frustration severing the softness of his affection for her and the freedom he had so often before encouraged.

'Could you not have come to me? Could you not have explained? Could you not have told me so that when the headmaster discovered me I could defend myself? So that I could make him believe *my* innocence?' His words were quietly spoken, but nonetheless whip-quick and just as painful, and Sofia resisted her body's urge to flinch.

'No and no,' she said sadly, because in truth— she still could not. She knew that the excuses she had presented to him, while very much real, were not the whole story. And she counted on his anger as much as her hope for his understanding—because if he *was* angry he might not see the gaping holes in what she had told him.

'Would you make the same decision again?'

He almost wished he could recall the words the moment that they left his lips. But he knew he needed to hear her answer as much as he needed her to say them. If she said no, then he might try to find a way out of this, to extricate himself from his path of revenge. It was as if there was a tide between them, pushing one way and pulling another. He felt like a man drowning, knowing that one push of the ocean would take him to the depths, one pull could see him back to shore, to safety, to a future he could have only prayed for.

As if Sofia felt that same tide, that same sense of the precipice before them, she turned to him, finally facing him, drawing herself up to her full height, her chin angled up as if to meet an oncoming army.

'There was never a choice. For my country, for my duty, yes. I would do it again in a heart-beat.'

Had she known that was the moment she might have been able to save herself from what was to come, she might have answered differently, he thought. But she hadn't. Instead, she only confirmed the words he needed to hear.

He pressed away the excuses she had given him about their time together, the slow erosion that had begun against the bedrock of his need for revenge. The image she had woven between them of a young woman trapped within a gilded cage of duty as she battled the natural, sprite-like instinct within her. Of a reckless young girl, ignorant of the consequences of her actions. His determination had begun to give...to loosen its grip around his plans and his feelings for her.

But Sofia's decisions that night had put into motion a chain of events that had led him and his mother to such pain... Had he stayed at the school, gone on to university, his mother would not have had had to work every back-breaking moment of those first five years alongside him, pouring their blood, sweat and tears into the very earth that eventually repaid them. But not without cost. His mother's heart attack could have been prevented. The bright, determined, loving woman he knew had been transformed into a vulnerable, weakened, pallid imitation of herself. And it had only been by nearly losing everything again that he'd been able to fund her treatment. But he could have done better. He could have taken his mother away from that hardship, from that life-or-death battle, had it not been for Sofia.

It took him a moment to realise that the buzzing wasn't just in his ears, but that of a mobile phone nestled on her dressing table.

'Do not answer it,' he commanded darkly. They were not done yet.

He watched her take in the number on the screen.

'I have to.' And for the first time after these ten years of absence he saw fear in her eyes and, speaking into the phone, she asked, 'What's wrong?'

CHAPTER SEVEN

HE HAD MADE Sofia wait while he quickly showered and changed. When she had insisted she needed to go *now* he had refused, firmly stating that five minutes would do no harm. And she hadn't been able to tell him why he was wrong. Bound by secrets she bitterly resented.

She had tried to walk out, but he had caught her arm and ordered her to take a breath. A breath? Even now she felt she hadn't inhaled once since hearing her mother's desperate pleas on the phone. He had dogged her steps as she had tried to leave without him, leaving muttered words like 'stubborn' and 'pig-headed' in their wake.

She scanned her mind for her father's routine. For something that would perhaps explain what could have happened to make her mother beg for her presence.

'You need to come here. Now. Please, Sofia.'

Panic was a feral thing, eating up the small, dark, cramped space of the limousine whisking her away to the small estate where her mother and father lived. Between her fear and Theo's brooding presence, she could barely move. It pressed in around her as she clutched the silk of the trouser suit at her thigh.

'I'll ask again—'

'And I'll say again, Theo, I cannot tell you what's going on. I don't even know.' And she hated the helplessness of her words and the truth in them. As the car drew up to the entrance to her parents' home, she commanded him to stay in the car.

And, for once, he must have seen the seriousness of the situation and listened.

Leaving him leaning against the limousine, the early morning sky barely touched by the light of the sun's rays, Sofia raced through the halls, the bodyguard who had ridden with the driver flanking her side.

One floor down from her parents' living quarters and she could already hear the muffled sounds of her father's anger. Her speed picked up, nearly causing her to stumble at the top of the marble stairs. She rushed through the heavy wooden doors, partly open as if ready for her arrival.

'Get your hands off me. Do you not know who I am?' her father demanded, his face red with anger and frustration.

'Of course they do, Frederick.' Her mother's gentle, soothing tone was doing nothing to calm her father's fury.

The sight of her father's frail old body being restrained by two men was almost enough to bring a cry to Sofia's lips. The skin on his arms loose, as if he were a puppy, still yet to grow into himself. Was this growing old? Sofia wondered. Reverting to a childlike state of tantrums, and folds of paper-thin skin?

'Sofia!' her father cried. 'Make them see. Make them see that they have to let me go. I need to speak to the council. The Prime Minister wants to raise the duty taxes on the…on the…' Becoming even more frustrated with his lack of memory, he growled, pushing and pulling against the two men restraining him.

Sofia didn't know where he was in his mind, but it wasn't now. The Prime Minister had greater things to deal with at the moment than raising duty taxes on anything, so it must have been some years ago.

'Papa, it's okay. We'll speak to him later. It's four o'clock in the morning, and he'll still be asleep. There's time, Papa.'

'No, there isn't,' he said, almost succeeding in throwing off one of the men. Sofia took a step back instinctively, hating the familiarity of the fear thrumming her pulse like a guitarist. Once again she rubbed at her forearm, at the place where a similar night had caused her father to accidentally fracture her arm and two ribs. She'd never forget the look of shock and confusion in her father's eyes as he'd utterly failed to grasp what he had done. It was a terrible thing to fear her own father.

'It's you, isn't it?' he demanded now, bringing her back to the present with a thump.

'What, Papa?'

'*You're* keeping me from him. You only want the throne for yourself. You've been…poisoning me. Whispering evil into my courtiers' ears. You want me gone.'

'Papa, that's not true,' Sofia said, gently, knowing that any trace of concern or upset only made him worse. Everything in her cried, *no*.

Proclaimed that she had never wanted it. 'This country needs you. *I* need you.'

'You never needed me,' he growled. 'Running around the castle like some pixie. Desperate to run off with that Greek boy and turn your back on us all.'

The stark irony struck home for Sofia, but she tried instead to cling to the quickly changing direction of his chain of thought, so easy to flip between her wanting the throne and wanting to throw it away.

'We should have let you go to him. You will be the death of this country. You were never fit to rule,' he cried as one of the carers administered an anti-psychotic drug. For them to be doing this now meant that they must have been struggling with him almost since he'd left the engagement party. Sofia knew they would have tried everything else.

'I know, Papa,' she couldn't help but admit as he somehow drew out her greatest fears. 'But I'm trying. I really am.'

As the two men assisting her father settled him gently back into a chair, her mother watched her with large, shimmering eyes.

'Sofia—'

'It's okay, Mama, I know. I know he doesn't mean it,' she lied as she turned away. Fear, sadness, loss, grief, it all pressed against her skin like little pin pricks, drawing blooms of invisible blood that left her feeling drained and exhausted.

Theo was watching the sun rise slowly over the forest surrounding the estate, the scent of pine and earth slowly unfurling from the ground in the gentle heat of the early morning. He relished that almost sappy resin taste and he tried to combine grape lineages in his mind in an attempt to distract himself from Sofia's revelation only an hour before.

He could tell that she had been giving him some truths. There was definitely something she was holding back, but…tiny tendrils of doubt about that night were corroding his fierce belief that she had purposefully set him up. They spread through his chest and tightened around his heart. Because just beneath that erosion was something deeper. Something darker and much more painful. Something that spoke of grief and the acrid taste of loss, one he remembered from years before meeting Sofia.

This odd sense that he'd lived with almost all his life…a barely audible whisper from an inner voice…*abandoned, again.*

Usually Theo could go for months without thinking of the man who had run from his mother, run from *him*. But ever since he had set out on this path of revenge he had always been a shadow at the periphery of Theo's vision, hovering, waiting. He remembered thinking as a child that it was only natural to think of his father and had half convinced himself that when he became a man, when he was eighteen, he'd somehow magically stop thinking of him. And to a certain extent that had been true. But only because of the damage limitation he'd been forced into following Sofia's actions. But here, in Iondorra, a place that—as far as Theo knew—his father had never set foot, a phantom pain was tingling, burning back into a life he thought he'd long snuffed out.

The creak of the large doorway at the top of the stone steps to the estate cut through the early morning air, and the moment he saw Sofia all thoughts fled his mind.

She looked…devastated. And it was horrible. Because he recognised that look. It was the look a child wore, no matter their age, when something truly awful was happening to a parent. He had seen it the moment he'd looked in the mirror after his mother had been taken to hospital.

He went to take a step towards her but held himself back. He wanted to take her in his arms, to hold her in the way that no one had held him that day. But he couldn't. Whether for her, or himself, he didn't know.

'Sofia?'

She descended the steps as if in a daze, her eyes unseeing, a numbness almost vibrating from her. This woman who had come alive in his arms, to his touch and his need only hours ago, was now hollow and absent. She came to stand before him, her head barely reaching his shoulders, so that he had to bend almost, to try and catch her sightless gaze.

'Sofia...' Her name almost a plea on his lips.

'Take me away, Theo. Please.'

Her request rang out over the years from all that time ago, the one he so desperately wanted to forget. They were words he had thrown back at her outside the Parisian ballroom. As if realising it herself, only after it was too late to recall them, she flinched. And then trembled.

'Entáxei.' He nodded. 'Okay,' he repeated for her benefit. 'We will go.'

And then he finally gave in to his desire, and pulled her into an embrace.

He had spoken briefly to the chauffeur of the change in plans and, while settling Sofia into the back of the limousine, Theo started on the phone calls needed. He'd pulled up the contact details for Sofia's personal secretary, ordered her to pack a bag and get it to the airport, and cancelled all Sofia's appointments for a week. He'd messaged Seb to make his apologies to Maria, realising that he'd be unable to make the exhibition he'd assured her he'd attend the night before.

As the limousine ate up the miles of smooth tarmac, he began to doubt his decision. He had never taken a woman back to his winery, to the place where his mother still lived. He wondered what she would make of the young princess and hated that he had once had the same thought, under the same circumstances. Hated the fact that he would introduce Sofia to his mother as his fiancée, only to abandon her at the altar. But he would. He must. Because only then would she realise just how much damage she had caused. Just how much hurt...

But as the limousine passed the castle and carried on, it failed to draw any kind of response from Sofia. The kind of numbness that she wore about her like a shield began to scare him. He remembered that feeling. That hopelessness that was so very easy to hide in. And he couldn't help the wish, the need, to protect her. To shelter her, even if it ran contrary to his own plans. She needed to get away. She needed to find herself again. And for the first time Theo began to doubt his plan for revenge.

Sofia opened her eyes and frowned in momentary confusion at the unfamiliar sights that met them. And then she remembered. Remembered the short flight on Theo's private jet, the drive to the exclusive marina, remembered the way that Theo had ushered her onto the small, but beautiful and most definitely luxurious, yacht and walked her straight into the cabin and ordered her to sleep.

Smooth mahogany surrounded her, and the

gentle, rhythmic sway beneath her called her back to that blissful slumber. Sofia wanted nothing more than to bury herself in the comfortable bedding, but unease told her she couldn't. Instinct, memories, they all crashed about her mind and she felt…it all. The numbness that had settled about her had finally worn off, and everything in her hurt. Ached. Her heart for her father, her head for Theo, and her bones, a deep, low ache—that was for herself.

Untangling herself from the nest of sheets wrapped around her body, she sat up, swung her legs over the side of the bed and saw a bathroom off to the left. Peeling off clothes that felt days old, she turned on the shower, not even giving it time to warm up. The shocking cool jets of water hit her skin like a slap, bringing her round, before the water warmed and comforted like an embrace.

By the time she had emerged from the bathroom, a selection of clothes were laid out on the bed. Someone had been in here while she was in the shower. Unseen hands had placed the clothes on the bed she had only just left, an unseen body had been barely a foot from hers while she was naked in the shower, and instinctively she knew. Theo.

While everything in her wanted to scrabble into the clothes and rush to find him, demand that he take her back to Iondorra, she forced herself to stop. To slow the speeding of her thoughts.

Take me away, Theo. Please.

She had asked him for this. She blinked back the tears that pressed against the backs of her eyes. She wouldn't cry. She wouldn't break. But she needed this. She needed him. Perhaps, instead of rushing back to be the princess everyone wanted, she could steal this time away, just for herself. Before duty fell like a tolling bell against her, before there was no turning back.

Dressed in a soft white linen shirt and blue capri trousers, Sofia left the bedroom and followed the small galley to the stairs in front of her. The sun beckoned from where it slanted through the shadows and Sofia realised she had no idea what time it was.

Bare feet took the metal steps up to the deck of the boat, and when she emerged into the light she looked up at the stunning sloping arc of a brilliant white sail against a cloudless azure sky. The yacht was small—as in not one of the monstrosities that many rich Europeans preferred—but long and incredibly beautiful.

She would have stopped at the sight of the sea, stretching out on all sides as far as the eye could see, the magnificence of the aquamarine water melding with the sky at an invisible horizon. She would have stopped to relish the heat of the sun as it drenched her in a comforting warmth, finding even the darkest places of her heart and healing it beneath the touch of the rays. But nothing, *nothing* compared to the sight of Theo at the helm of the boat tall and proud as he directed the wheel with just the palms of his hands, his fingers outstretched, his movements smooth and his gaze on the horizon...until he turned that powerful gaze on her.

The sight of him took her breath away. His dark hair was wind-tousled, and a pair of sunglasses may have masked his eyes, but they did nothing to conceal the proud cheekbones and jut of his strong jaw, a jaw covered in a dark brush of stubble that just cried out to be touched. His white shirt, buttoned low, exposed a chest of defined muscle, dustings of dark swirls hidden then revealed as the linen was shaken by the wind. Dark navy linen trousers hung low on his lean hips, and Sofia bit back a curse or a plea to the gods, she honestly couldn't tell any more. This was not the man-child she had fallen for in her youth, this was something altogether different. Her eyes ate up the changes in his body, the muscles corded in his forearms, the glimpses of the trail of hair leading below the beltline of his trousers, the wide stance of his bare feet planting him securely on the wooden deck, looking for all the world as if he were its ruler.

All these things she had not taken in when they had come together…she had been blinded by passion then, and now? Now he simply stood there bearing the weight of her scrutiny, allowing her to take her fill. It was too much, and she used the excuse of the bright sun to shield her eyes, breaking the connection that had bound them together for a moment.

'There are sunglasses over there. As well as some deck shoes, and in the cooler bag some breakfast.'

He gestured to the bench just across the deck and she found everything he had described.

'You need to use the sunscreen too,' he said as he secured the wheel, and disappeared below deck. She sprayed herself liberally with the lotion and donned the pair of beautiful sunglasses. She was just reaching into the cooler bag for a pastry when the scent of fresh coffee mixed with the sea-salt air. She nearly groaned out loud.

'Still drink coffee like a lifeline?'

'Yes,' she smiled, the feeling on her lips foreign and strange after the last few weeks. 'Can't live without it,' she said, gratefully accepting the mug he offered her. She watched as the sea wind whipped away the steam before it could swirl and dance above the dark liquid. Waiting for it to cool before taking a sip, she turned back to the horizon. 'Where are we?'

'The Ionian Sea.'

'It's beautiful.'

He nodded. And for a moment she was glad that they shared this silence. That he allowed her to listen to the sounds of the waves crashing against the hull of the yacht as it glided through the water, the whip and crack of the sail as it strained against the wind. She knew he had questions, she could feel them emanating from him, but that he had not yet voiced them was a pleasant relief.

'You got your boat,' she said with a sad smile, remembering their youthful plans of some impossible future, the ones made at the Swiss boarding school.

'Eventually,' he said, the word marshalled as if he'd wanted to say more.

Theo resumed his position behind the wheel and she folded her feet beneath her on the bench and sipped at her coffee, savouring the strong hit of caffeine and the smooth, sweet taste of the honey he had added. He remembered. She feared that he remembered everything.

It had been so easy to embrace her anger for him when he was being demanding, blackmailing and ruthless. Even when he had played her body's desires against her, plucking strings between them she had long thought severed. But now? Now she could see glimpses of the youth she had fallen for. His kindness, his acceptance of her, unlike anything she had ever known before then, and not since. Not even with Antoine.

If he had forced her to explain, shouted and demanded, she would have retreated. But in this space he gave her she found herself unfurling, expanding within it in a way that was all about her. Not about duty, or trade negotiations, not about a ring she would wear, or a role she would play for her country, for her family.

She couldn't remember the last time she had found time for silence, for herself and her thoughts. Even as she considered it, she felt the rising panic, the fear that something might be happening and she wouldn't know about it. As much as she hated it, she started to look for her phone.

'Your people have instructions to call me if they need you. They have the number of the yacht's satellite phone. Your mobile wouldn't have signal out here anyway.'

'But the meeting with the Hungarian ambassador—'

'Has been rescheduled.'

'And the interview with the *New York Times*?'

'And with *Paris Match*, the Iondorran prime minister, and the Swiss consulate. Your assistant is nothing if not efficient.'

'Yes,' she said, smiling at the thought of the apparently ruthlessly organised Theo dealing with her imperious assistant.

Instead of panic at the thought of all these

important events in her diary, she felt oddly relieved. For so long she had borne the brunt of her duties alone. For the first time it felt as if she had someone with her to share the load. Even if only to make the decision she would have known she had to make, but been incapable of making.

She caught sight of Theo's cocked head as he observed her. 'What?' she asked, feeling around her mouth and chin for flakes of the pastry that might have remained from her breakfast, oddly self-conscious under his scrutiny.

'You don't mind,' Theo stated.

'Mind what?'

'That I rearranged it all. I thought you would be hissing like a cat, threatening to throw me overboard and leave me behind in the sea as you hightailed it back to dry land and the nearest helicopter.'

'That's quite a long chain of thought you had there.'

'You were asleep for quite a while. I had enough time to imagine several possibilities.'

'There was definitely a time that tossing you overboard would have seemed like the right thing to do.' But her words reminded her that

that was almost exactly what she had done ten years before. And just like that the dam was lifted on the all the questions and all the curiosity about him she had hidden beneath layers and years of denial about him. About them. 'Can I ask…how did you get here? Your own yacht, a billion-euro wine industry…how did you make it happen?'

It hurt him, scratched at a wound that he had buried deep, that she had never thought to find out what had happened to him after that night. That she had so easily discarded him, even as he had at first stalked the internet to find any trace of news of her, as if knowing what she was doing would make the hurt and betrayal any less…or worse in some masochistic way. He pushed back his bitter thoughts and focused on her question.

'When I returned to my mother, she was already packing our belongings. Moritz, my mother's employer, was understanding, but his wife…not so much. She was furious that I had squandered the opportunity they had so generously provided and was determined that we should not bring further shame to their family name.' He still remembered the woman screeching at him and his mother from the top of the stairs, the way all the servants in the house had gathered to watch and the way, despite all this, his mother had placed her arms around him as if to protect him. He remembered the last look Moritz had cast him before they had left. One of pity, not shame, but full sadness and disappointment. He had never wanted to see such a look ever again.

'We returned to my mother's family because there was nowhere else to go. And it started up almost immediately. The snide comments, the years of resentment. My father's abandonment of his pregnant lover had consigned my mother to a life of shame. And the expulsion from school? Just compounded it.'

He couldn't look at Sofia as he told her this. He didn't want to see her expression, to see the truth of her feelings, so instead he looked out to the horizon as he steered the yacht to some indefinable destination.

'My mother had saved some money. Not a huge amount, but some. Enough to buy some land from her family. They were happy to get rid of it, and us, to the small home nestled in its boundary. The land was hard, dry and difficult and not one of them had ever been able to grow a thing on it. Their small winery was failing and, though they did not welcome her, they welcomed my mother's money, every last, single cent of it.' He couldn't help the bitterness in his tone. He hated them for what they had done to his mother. 'They could just as easily have given it to us because it had never made them any money and they hadn't used it for years, almost two generations. Which, ironically, is why it was much easier for me to work with it.

'For the first six months, I simply cleared the land. Each day, each night, bit by bit.' It was as if the mind-numbing work had been the only thing that had kept him going in those first few months where he'd been so raw it felt as if his very heart was exposed to the elements. The pain, the ache of her betrayal, the humiliation that he'd been taken in by her lies. But now, after all that had happened between them, he began to recognise something else in his feelings... the heartbreak that she had turned her back on him. That she had left him.

The jagged, wrenching pain that had made it almost difficult to breathe at times.

'My mother would help.' But only when she was feeling up to it, he now recognised. 'I hadn't realised how much knowledge I'd garnered from working in my mother's family's fields. The soil was good, having been left fallow for so long. I worked to ensure decent irrigation systems were in place to not undo all the work already achieved.

'Nikos, my neighbour, would watch from the seat in front of his home. He and my mother would sometimes share a coffee, and occasionally he'd call out suggestions. Mostly he was calling me several shades of a fool for doing it, but,' Theo said with a smile, 'it just made me more determined.

'Once the land was cleared, the night before I was to start planting Nikos called me over for dinner. Of course, his idea of food was three-day-old, tough-as-a-boot rabbit stew, but the *raki* was good. And so was a bottle of wine he produced from his cellar.

'He explained that it was his own wine, from a small variety of grape that had been growing on his land for generations. He'd never told my mother's family because in his opinion they were money-grabbing, pious *malakes*—his words—something we both agreed on. We stayed up until about three in the morning that night, drinking the few bottles of wine he'd produced. The problem with his grape was that, while it was hardy, it was also harsh. But it had potential. I think we must have talked about the characteristics of the grape, the barrel, the age, with more detail than scientists discussing genetic testing.

'So the next day, instead of planting pure *malagousia*, I took a risk. Half the land was the *malagousia*, and the other half was Nikos's grape. He didn't know the lineage of it, and his grandfather had probably forgotten the name of it. To Nikos, it was just wine. To me, it was the perfect grape to blend.

'The first two years were terrible.' He huffed out a reluctant laugh. It covered the sheer hours of the day he had spent outside, tending to those damn vines. But he wouldn't have changed it for anything. Those years were ones spent with his mother. Eating together, working together, laughing… Before it was nearly cruelly ripped away from him and he realised the true cost of the land.

Could he really lay the blame of his mother's illness at Sofia's feet? Could he hold to the anger that had driven him over the years and once again the moment she had refused to make a different decision? One that might have prevented his mother from ever having to experience such a devastating attack on her health?

In the silence that had settled between them he realised that the wind had picked up and set about securing the lines, considering whether or not he needed to bring down the sail.

'Did you ever think about giving up?'

'Every single hour of every single day,' he replied.

'But you didn't.'

'I wouldn't be standing here today if I had.'

'Do you…?' She paused and it drew his gaze to her. 'Do you ever wonder,' she pressed on, 'what would have happened if I had stayed? If perhaps…we could have had the life we'd hoped for?'

Whether he blamed her for what happened to his mother or not, Sofia had still not learned the consequences of her actions. Or she would never have asked that damn question.

'Never,' he bit out.

Her sigh was stolen by the wind, and he stalked the length of the deck, hoping that she would leave the conversation alone. But his hopes were in vain.

'I do. I thought I hadn't, but... I was just lying to myself. I did. Especially in those first few months. I'd wake up expecting to see you beside me, expecting to find my reality a dream, and my dream a reality.' The wistfulness in her voice cut him deep and he tried to ignore it, especially as she stood and made her way towards the side of the yacht. 'But perhaps,' she pressed on, 'it wouldn't have worked. It was a childhood fantasy. We couldn't have lived off dreams and desire. Reality would have always been waiting around the corner.'

'We would have made it work,' he said despite himself, finally looking back at her to find her standing at the side of the yacht, looking out at the sea.

'Really? The princess and...'

'The pauper,' he replied.

'You were never a pauper to me.'

'You were *always* a princess to me.'

The wind cracked the sail, lines creaking and groaning under the sway of the boat. The boom started to move, and terror raced through his veins. He shouted a warning to Sofia, but it was too late—she didn't hear him and, facing the sea, was ignorant of the oncoming danger. As the large wooden boom swung round with speed and weight he launched himself towards her, but was too far away. Sofia turned just in time to raise her hands to take the brunt of the hit, but not enough to avoid it. It caught her across the shoulder and thrust her into the sea.

CHAPTER EIGHT

THEO HATED HOSPITALS. He felt as if the sterile scent of them carried on the air entered his bloodstream and scratched at him from the inside out. He hadn't been back to this one since he had mortgaged his life to the hilt to fund his mother's operation, and he couldn't stop pacing, desperate to escape its walls, but unable to leave.

Lyssandros, the doctor who had become his personal physician of sorts, had kicked him out of Sofia's room for his assessment. Fear. It was a feral, living thing within him. Had he reached her in time? She hadn't been under the water more than five seconds before he'd dived in to reach her. He'd pulled her out, hauled her onto the deck and secured her as quickly as possible, before he dropped the sail and used the motor to get them back to land, breaking every maritime speed law around the world. A helicopter had met them at the marina, and staff had dealt with the vessel as he and Sofia were brought to the hospital.

He'd fought with Lyssandros not to leave her side, and even during the MRI scan he'd been in the small booth with the older man, ignoring the quiet discussions and assessments going on around him as he'd been unable to take his eyes from Sofia's small frame.

She'd been in and out of consciousness, babbling strange words that had scared him. She seemed to have been having an argument with someone about not wanting to leave. It had taken him a few rounds of the repeated conversation to realise that she wasn't imagining herself on the yacht with him, but at some long-ago point in time as she begged and pleaded to stay. He'd been able to do nothing but soothe and promise her that he wouldn't make her leave, but he doubted Sofia had heard him.

A sound at the door to her private room alerted him, and he spun round to find Lyssandros saying something to a nurse and dismissing her. Finally the older man turned to him.

'She is going to be okay.'

Breath whooshed out of Theo's lungs, and he

pinched the bridge of his nose as if it were the only thing holding him together. *Dóxa to Theó.*

'She has a concussion, unsurprisingly, so I want to keep her in overnight at least. Given her…status, it's possible that her people might want to move her—'

'They don't know about it yet.'

'Theo,' the doctor admonished. 'She's a princess, so her people, family, even her country, will want to know about this.'

'I'm not keeping it from them, but she needed this time away and—'

'Okay. It's your call, but if I'm asked—I had no idea who she was, other than your fiancée.'

'That's very ethical of you.'

Lyssandros smiled ruefully, though there was a hint of something in the other man's eyes that made Theo pause.

'What's wrong? You said she was okay,' Theo practically growled.

'She is, Theo. She is,' he said, placing a large hand on Theo's shoulder. 'But…look, I really shouldn't be saying anything, and I wouldn't… but it did give me some concern. It wouldn't have been picked up in a normal assessment, but you asked for every test under the sun, and

I did them.' Lyssandros led Theo a little further away from the nurses' station of the private wing Sofia had been brought to.

'I don't know what happened, only Sofia will be able to tell you that, but I've noticed a few injuries that would seem…unusual for a…for someone of her status.'

Theo frowned. 'Injuries? She usually has the reflexes of a cat.' Or at least she had done when they were at school. She had to have had, to get the headmaster's car on top of the sports hall. Except when she was distracted, as she had been on the yacht.

'It looks to have happened about a year, maybe a year and a half, ago, from the healing patterns, but around that time she took what must have been a pretty hard hit.'

'A hit from what?'

Lyssandros shrugged. 'She had a fractured ulna—' he gestured to his forearm '—and several broken ribs. I only mention it because it's uncommon for an adult to fracture only one of the two bones in the forearm, unless they are defending themselves.'

'Could she have done it horse riding?' Theo

queried, unable to quite understand how else it could have happened.

'I would have expected more damage, or less, depending.'

'You think it was a person. You think she was attacked.'

The older man nodded. 'As I said, it's only because of her status that I ask.'

Theo clamped his jaw on a million unasked questions, able to voice only one. 'May I?'

'Of course,' Lyssandros said, directing him to the door to Sofia's room.

Sofia's throat felt as if someone had poured sand down it, and she was half convinced that someone was trying to prise her head open with a jackhammer. When the door opened she managed to force her eyelids up enough to take in a figure wearing blue scrubs, and promptly closed them again. If she never saw another doctor again, it would be too soon. She wanted to go. Where, she wasn't sure. She didn't want to be back in Iondorra yet, and she wondered why Theo hadn't arrived to whisk her away. Had he left her? Had he finally decided that even his wine sales weren't worth this much hassle? The thought rocked her. Is this what he'd felt that night? Tears began to gather behind her closed eyes, but she wouldn't cry. Not in front of some stranger.

'Sofia…'

Her eyes flew open to find Theo coming to sit on the edge of the bed.

'Theo? What are you doing in scrubs?'

The rueful smile on his perfect lips did nothing to hide the fierce concern in his gaze. 'Lyssandros, the doctor, told me that I was getting his medical centre wet, so forced me to change into these,' he said, pulling distastefully at the blue material.

'Why were you wet?'

'Do you not remember? You fell into the sea, and I went in after you.'

'You did?'

'How else would you have got out?'

Sofia sighed. 'I'm surprised you didn't leave me in there,' she grumbled, frustrated with herself for not being able to put the pieces of what had happened together in her own mind. The doctor—Lyssandros—had explained that it was to be expected, and, as long as the confusion was only around the accident, he wasn't too concerned. All her tests had come back fine mostly. A bang to the head from the fall, a decent bruise to her shoulder from where the boom had caught her, but aside from that she'd been lucky.

'I was tempted. But the Greek government might frown at the manslaughter of a princess.'

'It would have been murder if you'd intentionally left me.'

'I'd have got away with it.'

A smile pulled at the corners of her mouth, just as a wave of exhaustion descended. 'When can I get out of here?'

'Tomorrow.'

'I hate hospitals. Can you sneak me out?'

'Lyssandros is as close as a friend, but even he's not taking risks with you.'

And neither am I. She felt his words, without him voicing them.

'I want to go,' she said, the words slightly slurred.

'I know. But you're safe here. I'm not going anywhere.'

Sofia tried to shake her head, but that hurt, and whatever she'd been about to say disappeared as she fell into the welcoming arms of sleep.

When she next woke, Sofia was thankful that the light didn't hurt her eyes any more, and she experimentally moved her head from side to side, relishing the fact that the jackhammer seemed to have given up.

She turned to find Theo in the chair beside her, his long legs thrust out in front of him, his head resting awkwardly on his fisted hand, elbow on the arm of the chair, and even in sleep the man looked incredible.

Long, midnight-coloured eyelashes dusted his cheeks, his dark hair tousled as if he'd spent the entire night thrusting his hands through it, and his jawline was now in serious risk of growing a half-decent beard. She kind of liked the look on him. It made him even more…just more.

When a nurse entered, Sofia thrust a finger to her lips, unwilling to wake him. The small, dark-haired woman smiled conspiratorially and came to her side to check the little monitor assessing her vitals.

'How are you feeling?' she whispered.

'Like I was struck off a yacht by a boom.'

She huffed out a small laugh. 'You should be

able to go soon. I'll have the doctor sign your discharge papers.'

'Thank you. I can speak to the Iondorran consulate and arrange for payment if—'

'No need. That's all been taken care of.'

At Sofia's frown, the nurse gestured to Theo, still asleep, and Sofia nodded and sighed. Not only had he rescued her from the sea, but also paid for her care. He was hardly getting his money's worth out of this, was he? A thread of sadness began to wind through her. Was that all there was between them or could there ever be more? she wondered. For years she had consigned thoughts and memories of him to a locked box in her heart. But now? She wasn't so sure any more.

It took them about an hour to get out of the hospital, partly because Sofia had wanted to thank everyone who had treated her. She made a mental note to ensure there was a donation to the hospital for their generosity and discretion. She couldn't express how relieved she was that there were no reporters camped out on the steps, that no international incident had been accidentally created. She wasn't naïve enough to think that it was out of respect for her, and could plainly see the adoration for Theo in the faces of most of the medical staff. He seemed to be on first-name terms with half of them, and it went beyond simple patronage, which confused her a little. Surely he had not worked up such strong bonds just in the time of her overnight stay there?

She waited on the steps to the hospital as a man brought round a large black Jeep and handed Theo the keys.

He ushered her into the passenger seat and went round to the driver's side, and got in.

'You're driving yourself?'

'Why? Did you want to?' he said with a laugh.

It stung. She couldn't help it. 'I can't.'

'When you're feeling better—'

'I can't drive,' she said angrily. It had been a small fight with her father, certainly not one of their greatest, but it had hurt just as much. Somehow it had become a larger symbol of all the things she wasn't allowed to do as a princess-in-waiting. But more than that, it had signified the true end to her freedom.

'I suppose you don't need to know how to drive,' Theo said as he pulled out of the hospital car park.

'No. I suppose I don't,' she replied bitterly, and almost growled when she saw Theo suppress a laugh. 'It's not funny.'

'I'm not laughing at you, Princess. It's just that you're cute when...when you're angry.'

'I'm not cute either,' and even she couldn't help but let loose a small laugh at the ridiculousness of her own sulk. This. This was what she had missed most about him. The ease. The ease and friendship that had turned into distrust and resentment the moment they had met again in Paris. 'Where are we going?' she asked to turn the wayward direction of her thoughts.

'Home. *My* home.'

Theo directed the car with the same ease with which he had directed the boat. He had always loved travel, movement, something that appeased the restlessness he'd always seemed to feel back in Greece. The freedom he felt at being in charge of his own destiny, especially having spent years at the whim of the elements and the vineyard. He couldn't imagine not being able to control that, and wondered whether that was what had made Sofia so bitter. Not being able to choose when and where and how she wanted to go.

He frowned as he remembered the thread of a conversation from the night in Monaco.

'I have no choice in this whatsoever.'

Casting an eye over to where Sofia slept, he felt unease stir in his chest. He hadn't given her a choice. Not really, no matter what he had said to her. Every single moment of that night in Paris, and then Monaco, had been carefully orchestrated to ensure Sofia's ultimate humiliation. But now? Was that still what he wanted?

He changed lanes and came off the motorway as they began to make their way through the Peloponnese countryside, travelling along the southern part almost to the border with Messinia.

Cypress and olive trees skirted the mountains in the distance, scarred with jagged lines of white stone and brown scrub, and through the open window the scent of home filled the Jeep. Large stretches of mottled green land were occasionally interrupted by red-roofed towns and he welcomed the sight of them. Arcadia might not be the typical tourist destination popular with travellers from across the world, as Athens and the islands were, but that just made it even more precious to him.

It had been hard hit in recent years, especially with so many of the younger generation leaving for America, or other parts of Europe, but its people were surviving, hard work and determination making the most of this place that could be made. He was pleased that his vineyard had grown to such an extent that he now employed almost half of the nearby town. The estate he and his mother had dreamed of building one day was now able to offer luxurious stays in the vineyard, wedding packages and tours, and the seven-course wine-tasting menu at the Michelin-starred restaurant enticed guests from all over the world.

He pulled off into the road that led towards the gated estate, slowing until the electronic security system at the side entrance recognised the car's plate, just as Sofia stirred from her sleep.

The gates opened and he guided the car down the long drive, the smooth turns allowing him to observe Sofia's eyes growing wide as she took in the large, sweeping vineyard to the left.

'This is...magnificent,' she sighed and he

couldn't help the swell of pride he felt deep in his chest.

'This is only a quarter of the vineyard. There is more to the back of the estate.'

'Where is…?' She trailed off as they rounded the last bend and the building before them rose up to greet them. 'Oh.'

He took in the sight of it as if with her eyes—eyes that had never before seen the estate. The large central building was almost monastic in design, built from reclaimed grey stone, and had sweeping archways that his mother had loved from the first sight of it. It provided the entrance as well as the large dining restaurant and access to the front half of the wine cellars below, the area that was available for guest tours.

The more modern annex off to the left provided views both front and back from large windows on three floors for each of the guest suites, all of the twenty rooms lavishly designed with en suite bathrooms big enough to house the first home he and his mother had shared on the land. One that was still tucked away at the back of the large property.

'Theo, this is incredible,' Sofia said as he

pulled up to the staff car park to the side of the building. He could tell from the number of vehicles in the guest parking area that they were at low capacity. He cast his mind over the appointments and remembered that the estate was winding down before a wedding booking in just two days' time.

She was out of the car before he was.

He watched her spin in a slow circle, taking in the view of the estate. 'Do you want to freshen up? There's—'

'No!' She turned, laughing. 'I want to *see*. I've been in bed for twelve hours or more, sleeping in the car for the last three, and now I want to move. Please? Show me?'

And he wondered when he'd ever really been able to deny her anything.

'I would love nothing more. But I intend to do it in something other than a pair of scrubs,' he said, pulling at the scratchy material of the blue top. 'It will still be there after a shower and a change of clothes. I promise.'

Sofia had been surprised by the sheer magnificence of Theo's vineyard. Oh, she'd known that he had made money from his business, clearly enough to gain entry to the society of the masquerade ball in Paris. As she cast her mind back she remembered his taunt about his billionaire status and couldn't help but marvel at what he'd achieved.

The marble flooring in the entrance to the main building was beautiful and shot with veins of dark green and black. She had watched, fascinated, as Theo had nodded to his employees on Reception, paused to ask after the father of one of the young girls manning the desk. It gave Sofia time to explore the room. She marvelled at the wooden bench that stretched the entire length of the room. On top were squares of slate, wedging wine bottles in between, with handwritten names and descriptions in italicised chalk. Beneath were large oak barrels that added a touch of authenticity as well as artistic integrity to the main hall.

When she turned she found Theo watching her, as if waiting for some kind of censure or disapproval. She sent him a reassuring smile, and he whisked her away to the private wing.

He had deposited her and her bag retrieved from the boat in a room most definitely fit for a princess. The large canopied bed had been an indulgence she had never personally given into, but loved the moment she set her eyes on it. Rustic luxury. She was surrounded by it.

The bathroom was something completely other. One entire wall was lined in antique mirrors, in front of which was a free-standing cast-iron bath. To the left was a large window that looked out on to a stretch of vineyard behind the property. She hung back slightly, wondering if she would be seen, but realised that from this height and distance only the birds would be able to spy her.

In the corner was a glass-fronted shower, large enough for two people...in her mind, two people that looked very much like her and Theo. A blush rose to her cheeks as her wayward imagination ran wild...a heady mixture of memory and fantasy, desire and need aching within her. When they had come together after the engagement party, anger and resentment had dominated despite her aching desperation to feel him. She wondered if that would be so now? If perhaps to make love to Theo would be different...

She turned the shower on and stripped off the clothes that clung to her aching body. She had said that she wanted to see the vineyard but knew that Theo had been right. She allowed the hot jets of water to ease the aches from the last few hours, gently washing her hair, careful of reawakening the dull ache from the fall into the sea. Scrubbing away the remnants of the salt water, she felt fresh, new and oddly happy.

Happy. She considered it. When had she last felt it? A small part of her was so sad that she couldn't remember when it had been. She padded into the bedroom wrapped in a towel and searched through the bag of clothes that had been packed for her by her assistant back in Iondorra.

Her fingers brushed something lacy, and with something like horror and fascination she produced a silk negligee fit for a honeymoon. Doubting very much that Theo had requested such a thing, she realised that her assistant had only packed what Sofia might have wanted for a last-minute getaway with her fiancé.

Because he *was* her fiancé. No matter how or why it had happened, it was the case. And she would be marrying him. But what would that marriage look like now? The start of their engagement had been all anger and vengeance, but somehow over the last few days that had changed, and it had morphed into something that she hardly dared to hope for.

Placing the negligee on the bed, she dug into the bag and produced a pair of tan high-waisted linen palazzo pants and a cream silk vest. With her hair still wet, she wound it into a knot and secured it high on her head.

She buckled a pair of brown leather low-wedge sandals at her ankles and, snagging the sunglasses on her way out, left her room and returned to the reception area, safe in the knowledge that Theo would find her there when he was ready.

When Theo found her, Sofia was leaning against the large domed archway, her slender hips shown to perfection by the trousers encasing her narrow waist, one ankle crossed over the leg bearing her weight, and the wind blowing the loosely tucked-in silk top. It was such a sight it gave him pause. Pause for what he was about to do, because he knew that he couldn't continue on his path of revenge without first finding out what had happened to cause the fracture of her arm and damage done to her ribs. Without finally getting to the truth of her.

The fierce streak of protectiveness that leapt to life in his chest at the mere thought of it shocked him with its intensity.

As if she sensed his presence, she turned, her face cast in a shaft of soft sunlight peering through the shadows of the cool reception, and her smile caught him low in his chest. He stalked towards her, fighting with his desire to haul her into his arms and kiss her. Kiss her in a way he hadn't since he was seventeen. Kiss her in the way he should have that night in Iondorra.

Shame filled him as he thought of how they had come together that night. As if they were combatants on a battlefield, rather than lovers on a bed of silk sheets and roses. As he reached her, she turned her face towards him as if waiting for that same kiss. But instead of doing what he so desperately wanted to do, of taking what he so desperately needed, he offered his arm and escorted her away from the reception and away from his wayward thoughts.

Theo was thankful that she made easy small talk as they walked towards the rows of vines that made up the vineyard. Questions of what types of grape, how long they took to grow, when he had first known that he wanted to develop wine… All things he had answered a million times and knew by heart. And, if she noticed that he was distracted, she was restrained enough not to mention it.

Finally, as they drew to the furthest point from the estate, he turned to her.

'What is it?' Sofia asked. 'You've had something on your mind for a while. Ask.'

As if it were that simple. As if she would not deny him anything.

'At the hospital, I asked Lyssandros to run every possible test he could think of. The thought…the possibility that you were hurt—'

'I'm fine, Theo. Truly. Look,' she said, shaking her head from side to side in a way that made him wince, even without the possibility of concussion. She laughed. The sound should have soothed him, but it didn't.

'Lyssandros is a very professional man, but he also has a huge heart. He was concerned by… He saw there were fractures, from a previous injury. Did someone hurt you?' he asked, his voice drawn and gravelly to his own ears. Watching her closely, he saw the way she paled, the way her cheeks lost their rosy glow, her eyes filled with shadows and she made to turn away. Before she could, his hand snuck out and gently grasped her chin, guiding it back to him, snaring her gaze with his.

'Please. Don't hide from me in this. I need to know.'

She pulled a breath into her lungs, but it seemed to get caught there, the slight stutter in her breathing enough to tell him that he really did need to know. As if unable to bear the weight of his gaze, she cut her eyes to the ground.

'Sofia, whatever it is…whoever it was… If it was your husband—'

'No!' she cried, cutting him off mid-sentence. 'No,' she said again, more gently, more softly. 'Antoine never raised a hand to me. Ever.' He watched her pause and take another deep breath. 'My father isn't well.'

It was not what he'd expected her to say, but he silenced his inner thoughts and allowed her to continue.

'He hasn't been for…some time. I…we, the palace, have been sworn to secrecy, for fear of it destabilising the future of Iondorra.'

'What is wrong with him?'

'He was diagnosed with early onset dementia.'

She started to move away from him then and in the space between them his suspicions began to grow, like roots from somewhere deep within him, reaching towards the light, towards the truth.

'When?'

'When what?'

'Don't play games with me, Sofia—when was he diagnosed?'

'Just before I was taken out of boarding school.'

A curse fell from his lips as he stared to rearrange the past to fit with what she was now telling him.

'The night that I was supposed to meet you, he and my mother came. At first, I thought they'd found out somehow. About you, about the pranks… But it was worse than that. They explained what the diagnosis meant, that in time he would begin to lose more and more of his memory, of himself. I couldn't see it. This man, this powerful, loving, larger-than-life ruler of an entire country…it wasn't possible. Or at least that is what I thought at the time.

'He was only fifty. There should have been

years before I needed to assume the royal responsibilities I was so ready to reject. But there was no one else. I was going to have to wear the crown, I was going to have to learn to be the ruler of Iondorra, and I couldn't do that to you.'

'*To* me, or with me?' he demanded.

'Neither,' she said, shaking her head helplessly. 'We were children, Theo. You...you had your whole life ahead of you, to do what you wanted to do, to be who you wanted to be. And who you are now is incredible,' she said, her eyes large and bright in her eyes.

Theo shook his head against her words, against the thought that she had been right. All this time he'd blamed her, hated her...

'Why didn't you tell me this?' he demanded, pain and anger making his words harsh on the soft summer breeze.

'I couldn't. Don't you see? No one could know of my father's diagnosis. The risk to the country, to its finances and its people...it was just too great. So I was taken back to Iondorra, and spent the next few years cramming in as much of the knowledge of a would-be ruler in the shortest amount of time possible.

'It's not like in the movies, where a simple

makeover is enough. My wayward recklessness needed to be ironed out of me at every turn. It took years learning the rules, etiquette, languages, diplomacy needed to ensure the success of the throne. All the while keeping this secret. One that ate away at me each day.

'Could you imagine what the world's press would do with a sniff of hereditary early-onset dementia in the Iondorran royal family? They are tough enough on debauchery, let alone something as devastating as a genetic disease.'

'You have been tested.' It was a statement rather than a question.

'Yes. I don't have it. The gene. Not that it means I won't develop the same condition, but the chances are significantly less.'

'So the injuries you sustained...'

She looked up at him then, her eyes matching the blue depths of the sky, large enough for him to see the sorrow, the pain and the frustration.

'My father had a bad turn. He...we'd been managing his condition fairly well up until that point. But that night, he was...not the man I knew. He had been restless and demanded to see me. He wanted to know how I was managing a negotiation with the Hungarian consulate, but…that had been months before. The negotiation done and dusted. Only…he didn't seem to remember that. He became frustrated and angry, furious even. I tried to calm him, but he saw it somehow as an attack, and he… he was just defending himself,' she tried to explain. 'The horror in his eyes, the moment he realised what he'd done…the guilt, shame…all of it was—' she paused as if searching for the right words '—so awful.'

Theo tried to shake his thoughts into clarity, as if they were flakes within a snow globe, hoping that they'd settle into some kind of sense. But no matter how they ebbed and flowed, all he could think of was that he believed her. That he could see the pain and hardship she'd been through. But, worse than that, he'd begun to feel as if his anger and hatred towards her for what happened to him and his mother was masking something else. He felt as if he'd been hit by an avalanche of guilt and it was covering everything.

A huge, fat, tear-shaped raindrop thudded on the ground beside his feet. Then another, and another. In just seconds, the heavens had opened as if they were crying for them, for him, for a pain he couldn't yet express.

Sofia looked up at him, seemingly heedless of the rain pouring down on her, and reached her hand to his hard jaw.

'I'm so sorry. I'm so, so sorry,' she said, her voice barely a whisper amongst the pounding of the rain on the earth beneath them.

And in that instant, he honestly didn't want to hear anything more. No words, no explanations, no apologies. He reached for her as his lips seized her with the same ferocity as that of the storm, drew her towards him as if she were the breath he needed to exist.

His tongue delved between soft, sweet lips and it wasn't enough. He wanted it all. Desire drenched him as surely as the rain as he felt her body mould against his own, the firm jut of her breasts against his chest, and he pulled her even closer, his thumb tracing down her slender neck to her ribcage, snagging on her hip and anchoring her to him.

She gave him everything he demanded, gave herself completely over to him, until she began to tremble, and in turn he finally felt the stinging cold of the summer storm. He broke the kiss, glancing towards the main building, which was too far away. He grasped her hand.

'Come with me,' he said, asked, possibly even pleaded in that moment, as he took them towards the summer house nestled on the boundary of the vineyard.

CHAPTER NINE

SOFIA COULDN'T STOP SHAKING, even as she took a second step and a third into the small beautiful wooden summer house. She knew it wasn't just because of the rain. She had never told anyone about her father. No one outside her mother, or her father's carers. She had put her trust in Theo. And it had been terrifying, but she wouldn't take it back. Not for a second.

She had seen him war with the truth of her words, with what it had meant for them all those years ago, and possibly even what it meant for them now. But she didn't want to think about her father, or Iondorra. No. Now she wanted to lose herself, or find herself, she couldn't say.

She turned to see Theo standing in the glass-fronted doorway, the fierce sky pouring rain down on the vineyard, casting everything else in dull grey, but Theo in full, bright glory. He looked like an avenging angel, dark hair even blacker than the night, his clothes drenched and clinging to the dips and hollows of his body as if he were a thing to be worshipped.

As he stalked towards her she fought the instinct to step back. She wouldn't hide from this any more, hide from her desire, she was now focused on him completely, the one man, the *only* man she'd ever wanted. The only man who had seen her for who she truly was, before duty had moulded her into something new. Something other.

They reached for each other at the same time, colliding in need and passion and want. She felt the beat of her heart leap as his lips crashed against hers, as his hands cradled her head, angling her in a position that felt as much like surrender as it did defiance. He thrust his tongue into her mouth, filling her, consuming her, and she needed it. It was too much. She felt like laughing, like crying, as if she simply didn't know which way was up or down any more, all she knew was him.

Her hands flew to his shoulders, large, solid, bigger than the breadth of her hands. Her nails dug into the thin, wet material covering his body and she wanted to feel skin, needed to. Her hands went to the buttons of his shirt, but the tremors shaking her body made her actions too slow.

He released his hold on her, and she swayed from the loss, the support, the anchor of his body. She watched as he tore apart his shirt, buttons flying and scattering on the wooden floor, marvelling at the smooth planes of his chest, the soft whorls of damp hair clinging to a deeply tanned torso. As he reached for her she gazed, fascinated by the cords of muscles rippling from the movement, and reached out a hand tentatively. She wanted to touch, needed to, but...

He swept up her hand in his and placed it on his chest, on his heart, and looked at her with such intensity she could hardly bear the weight of it. She felt the beat of his heart, powerful, strong and fast, raging in time with her own. His skin was hot beneath her cool palms and she shuddered, wanting to feel that heat wrapped around her, fill her, warm the places of her that had been left cold the moment she left him standing at the boarding school all those years ago.

It was then that she knew what it felt like to be in the eye of the storm—the moment of shocking quiet stillness while chaos raged around them. The moment that life as she knew it would change. She knew that he was giving her this. This moment to walk away. To stop. But she couldn't, wouldn't.

She reached for him then, raising to her tip-toes to reach that proud, utterly sensual mouth of his, desperate to feel it against her own. Her hands explored his rain-slicked skin, delighting in the feel of his strength, his power. His hands cupped her backside and he lifted her off her feet, her legs wrapping round his lean waist as if they'd always been meant to be there.

He backed up and sat them down on the large summer lounger, her knees anchoring against his hips, as he pulled at her silk top, freeing it from the waistband of her trousers, pulling it over her head and tossing it aside, snagging on the pins that held her hair in place and pulling it free as her long blonde hair hung down in thick, wet ropes about her shoulders. He stopped then and stared.

'You are so beautiful,' he said, placing open-mouthed kisses along her neck as she shivered under the feel of his tongue on her skin. His hands cupped her breasts, his thumbs brushing her nipples, stiff with pleasure, and Sofia's head fell back, relishing the feel of him, of what he was doing to her body, as he honoured her with his touch.

She gasped when he took her nipple into his mouth and sucked, teasing her with his tongue, his arm around her waist holding her in place against the onslaught of desire that threatened to overwhelm her.

Unconsciously she rocked against his lap, the hard ridge of his arousal at her core making her slick with need as much as the groan that fell from Theo's lips.

'You're killing me here,' he said, the words half huffed out on a laugh.

He pulled back, looking at her, his gaze taking its fill of her. He reached behind her, and began to unbuckle her sandals, first one, then the other. He took her foot in one hand and firmly pressed the entire length of the arch of each foot, sending delight and pleasure through her. He caressed her ankles beneath the wet linen of her trousers, encased her calf in powerful, calloused hands, rough against smooth, sensations overwhelming her. She moaned out loud and he cursed, wrapping one strong arm around her as he twisted them in an embrace and turned her back to the seat.

Her fingers fought against his to undo the button of her trousers, and, once done, he peeled them from her, slowly, languorously as if enjoying the unveiling as much as anything else. She couldn't find the words to describe him. He was glorious. Shirtless, his chest was magnificent, and she watched with the same delight as he kicked off his shoes and removed his trousers without taking his eyes from hers once. She almost shook her head against the impossibility of seeing him standing there naked, proud, and every inch her fantasy. She began to tremble again, not with cold, not from the elements, but from the sheer virility that was Theo, the magnetism, just him.

Theo stood naked before the most beautiful woman he'd ever seen. There she was, laid out before him like the last meal he'd ever taste, and he hovered on the brink of something indefinable, as if he didn't know where to start.

He wrapped a hand around her ankle and gently pulled her so that she almost lay flat. He lifted her foot, pressed kisses against the delicate arch, the inside of her ankle, he made his way slowly, languorously along her calf, spreading her slightly to allow the space for his own body, as he trailed open-mouthed kisses over her thigh and upwards to the hollow at her hip. Her body quivered beneath his lips, and he dusted the gentle swell of her stomach with his tongue. He kissed over her ribcage, and bit back a smile as she twisted and bucked as if as overwrought by the pleasure they built between them as he was. He kissed between her perfect breasts as he moulded them with his hands, each kiss driving him closer to the brink of need and desperation. This wasn't the angry coupling from the other night, this was honour, and respect, and desire building pathways to his heart that he'd never imagined.

He wanted to give her the greatest pleasure, as if he could make up for the ills he had thought her guilty of, the ills he had almost wreaked upon her. Because he realised now that he could not go through with his plan...he could no longer leave her at the altar humiliated and abandoned. Because beneath the ache and sting of what he had felt for Sofia was something deeper, darker and something he did not yet want to face.

She reached for him, as if pulling him back to the present, pulling him back to her, and he was more than willing to take the comfort she offered, even as he realised that it should have been the other way round. After what she had told him, it should be him soothing her hurts.

Leaning on his forearm, he looked down at her, the damp golden ropes of her hair framing her face, the exquisite perfection of it, and the way her head cocked to one side elongated her neck made him yearn to devour her there, the pulse point, the connection to life, the flutter there speaking of her need for him.

Wide, round, azure-blue eyes stared up at him in complete trust, and part of him wanted to shy away from that gaze, from the hope and innocence within it. Instead he followed the trail of his hands with his eyes as his fingers traced the outline of her ribcage, the pad of his thumb dipping into the hollow at her hip, his hand delving beneath her, curving around her backside to pull her against him, their centres flush, their cores both throbbing with need, and he released her only to sweep his hand low across the gentle swell of her abdomen and between her legs to find the place that drove her wild with ecstasy.

His thumb caressed and played with her clitoris, the sounds of her need rising higher than the pounding of the rain against the wooden roof of the gazebo, ringing vibrations over his skin through to his very soul. This time he would not tease her, keeping her at the brink of an orgasm. No, he would drench her in as much pleasure as she could take, and then more.

He thrust into her with his fingers, feeling the walls of her body clench around them, again and again, all the while his body aching with need, an ache he felt he deserved to bear even though it was Sofia that cried out, Sofia's body that trembled beneath him, incomprehensible words begging and pleading falling from her perfect lips. He wanted to kiss them, to consume them with his own mouth, but he couldn't, wouldn't, stop watching how beautiful she was when she came apart in his arms.

It wasn't enough, not nearly enough. Sofia's body, still vibrating with the power of the orgasm Theo had pulled from her very soul, still wanted more. It wanted him and wouldn't be denied. Her hands reached for him, drawing him down upon her, and finally, as if they were puzzle pieces fitting together, she felt some kind of completion as he placed the tip of himself at her core, and as he thrust into her deeply she felt stripped bare, vulnerable and powerful at the same time, as if she had stolen something from him to bolster her own sense of self.

The thickness of him filled her completely, the smooth hardness within her she was afraid she was already addicted to. He reached beneath her, bringing their bodies to a place where he could drive into her with more power, more delicious friction, just more… And she gasped, the air almost lodging in her throat, her heart as they became joined at the deepest, closest part of themselves. Was this what she had turned away from all those years ago? This impossible to describe sense of rightness, sense of wholeness? It was the last thought she had as he drove her closer and closer to a second orgasm—and with no need for silence or discretion, with no need for secrecy she cried out her release into his mouth as his lips came down on hers with the same desperation, the same craving that she could no longer resist.

Walking back through the vineyards as the sun hung low in the sky, slashes of pink against the cornflower-blue creating a stunning sight, Sofia wondered at the warmth and safety she felt as Theo wound his arm around her waist, holding her to his side. Their clothes still damp from the rain storm that had caught them by surprise, she almost welcomed the rough feeling, knowing what pleasures it had led to. She knew that they would have to return to Iondorra tomorrow for the charity gala, which—even though only a week before their wedding—she wouldn't have cancelled for the world. Her role as patron for Gardes des Enfants d'Iondorra—a charity that supported child carers—had given her the first glimpse she'd had that her royal status could be a positive thing—could help and support something both wider and yet smaller and more immediate than anything her 'duties' could effect.

But for the first time she was torn. Torn between her duty and wanting to stay here in this magical bubble where the outside world didn't exist and where she and Theo were finally feeling as one, feeling right, as if this was how it should have been all along.

She laughed out loud, then, when she felt the gentle vibrations at her side from the phone in Theo's pocket—both at the feeling, and the contradiction of her thoughts of it just being the two of them cut off from the rest of the world. But when Theo joined in her breath caught—she had forgotten what he had looked like when he smiled, when they laughed together, and the sight was...incredible, full of hope for the future and the pull of nostalgia from the past.

'Nai?' he said, still laughing as he answered the phone.

Trying not to feel a little stab of hurt when he pulled away from her to speak into his phone, she forced herself to tune out the conversation and turned her mind to tomorrow...to the future. With him? Married to Theo Tersi? After all that had happened to them years ago, and since?

Unconsciously she had walked forward, tracing her steps back towards the stunning hotel hidden amongst the rows and rows of grapevines that stretched as far as she could see. The little narrow lanes created between them were barely enough for one person to step along.

She felt Theo behind her, the heat of him, the awareness…

'That was my mother,' he announced, disconnecting the phone.

'Oh?' She'd hoped her word sounded nonchalant rather than…what, worried? Intrigued? How much did his mother know about what had happened between them? What on earth must she think of her?

'She has invited us for dinner this evening. If that's okay?'

Sofia pulled every one of her concerns beneath the well-worn mask she used almost daily for her royal duties. 'Of course that's okay. I would love to meet her,' she said genuinely, all the while hoping that Theo's mother didn't hate her quite as much as she hated herself for what she had done to Theo all those years ago.

Theo had never, ever introduced his mother to anyone he had been intimately involved with. He knew that she refused to read the articles written about him in the last two years, and only now did he realise how ashamed he felt of them. Ten years ago, he had intended to bring Sofia to his mother and...what? It was only now that he was beginning to realise that what Sofia had said on the boat was true. That what they had shared at school had been the stuff of fantasies and impossible dreams. Had she perhaps not been a princess it might have been different, but even then, Theo wasn't quite sure.

He almost laughed, bitterly, at the thinly fabricated future they had concocted in their minds. Even had she not been a princess, even with the scholarships, the reality was that he would have had to take one, maybe two jobs to pay for living expenses. He would have struggled just as much as he had in reality, but with her by his side. He would have spent hours, days away from her, and possibly in the end either resented that he wouldn't have been able to provide the life he had wanted for her, or, worse, her. And she? Would have been ruined by the hard life he would have taken them to. And he couldn't shake this feeling that perhaps what had happened was how it had been meant to be. That the very reason he'd been able to achieve such impossible success was the drive and determination that had fuelled him all these years. These thoughts struck a cruel blow as they reached the door to the small house on the border of his land.

He'd tried so many times to entice his mother to a grander home, an easier home perhaps on one floor, with cleaners, and staff even, but she had refused, loving the little home that they had first shared when he'd initially bought this land.

Before he could even raise his hand to the door, it swung open and he was instantly enveloped by his mother's small frame and a stream of adoring, loving Greek spoken so quickly, even he only picked up on half the words. Within seconds both he and Sofia were being practically dragged over the threshold, straight into the small kitchen full of smells that instantly made his mouth water, and heart lurch with memories of the past.

He looked at Sofia standing in his mother's kitchen—a smile one of her biggest and brightest as she stood there in a pretty summer's dress. She had told him, every inch the royal, that she refused to meet his mother in wet clothes, and they had returned to the rooms in the hotel to shower and change before coming here. But now—with no trace of any etiquette, no royal greeting on his mother's behalf, simply welcomed through the door and into the kitchen, Sofia seemed happier than she had in all the days he'd spent with her.

Aggeliki was tactile, even for a Greek mother, and he marvelled at how Sofia—usually protected by a dozen bodyguards from anything even close to physical contact—was taking all the touching and hugging. His mother was asking her about how she liked the vineyard, and he was about to translate, when Sofia, along with a surprising amount of gesturing, managed to explain that she liked it very much. In Greek. When had she learned Greek? he wondered. She was doing fairly well, but every now and then had to defer to him for the translation of a few words, and after he'd warned his mother to slow down they seemed to be able to understand much of what was said between them. Their evening became a strange mix of Greek, English and the occasional French, when even English wouldn't do.

They sat outside at a wooden table beneath a pergola almost buckling under the weight of the stunning bougainvillea they had planted when they had first bought the land. Aggeliki had lit citronella candles the moment she had seen Sofia's pale skin, knowing that the mosquitos would love nothing more than to feast on the perfect blood in her veins, and the lemony scent hung in the warm night air as they feasted on the numerous dishes Theo's mother had produced.

He watched his mother and Sofia, heads bent together almost conspiratorially, and realised that he could not go through with his plan for revenge. He had told Aggeliki that he was to be married, but had refused to sink so low in his mother's expectations as to admit the truth behind his actions. He couldn't help but feel a sense of rightness as he watched the two women together, forging a relationship in the way he'd once imagined ten years ago.

He hadn't missed the way that Sofia had been nervous about meeting his mother, but hadn't managed to reassure her that she didn't have to worry, that he'd never revealed the source of his shame. Because he'd been so consumed by the way the blame he'd laid at her feet—which had once been on such on solid ground—was now shifting.

Sofia sat back in her chair, more full of food

than she could ever remember being in her entire life. She had tried to help Theo's mother take the plates away, but she had shooed her with hand gestures, firmly keeping her in the seat, and Sofia had reluctantly stifled her manners.

For just a moment it was her and Theo, his brooding gaze on her, glimmering in the darkness—the thin shadows cast by the little citronella candles enough to create warmth but not quite illumination. Not that she needed it. She knew every millimetre of his face, his features etched in her heart for ever ten years before—she'd only had to let herself remember them. For one moment, barely the space of a heartbeat, there was peace between them. Peace and something she'd dare not put a name to. Because if she lost it again, she didn't think she'd survive.

Aggeliki returned to the table with even more food, this time the scent of sweetness hitting Sofia hard and making her mouth water.

She laughed, 'What is all this?'

'This is dessert!' Theo's mother proudly claimed as she put down the tray covered with enough sweet treats to feed an army. She also noticed on the tray a small plate with a number of pills and frowned as she watched Aggeliki take them with a mouthful of water in between each one. She raised a brow at Theo, who had yet to take his eyes from his mother, now swallowing down the last one, but Aggeliki must have caught the look.

'It's okay,' she said, rubbing warmth into Sofia's cold hand. 'It's nothing. I am fine,' she said with smiling reassurance, but it did nothing to ease the concern building in Sofia's chest.

'My mother...she had a heart attack and was treated and is now—as she says—better than ever.' Sofia didn't call him on the brief pause that spoke of his own concern, instead focusing on what she needed to know.

'When?'

Theo shrugged and shook his head. But she wouldn't let it go that easily.

'When did it happen?' she asked, purposefully gentling her tone.

'Five years ago,' he said, refusing to meet her gaze.

Something cold and hard twisted in her chest

and ached for him, for his mother, for her own selfish actions. From what he had told her earlier in the vineyard, he'd barely won his first vintner's award. He may have had some success at that point, and she didn't know much about the Greek healthcare system, but knew enough. Enough that meant it would have nearly crippled them financially, especially with a fledgling business underway, not to mention the hard work and struggle that it must have taken to be torn between a sick parent and full-time duty. Yes. She knew enough about that to know what it must have cost him.

She searched her mind for the words that would explain how she felt, how truly sorry she was, but they wouldn't come. They didn't have to. Finally Theo met her gaze and she knew that what he saw in her eyes was enough. He nodded, as if he'd understood, all the while his mother explaining the different types of dessert she wanted Sofia to try. And, as full as she was, Sofia would take a bit of each and every one of them.

This time, when it came to clearing the table, she ignored Aggeliki and helped the woman back into the small kitchen with the empty plates and coffee cups from the end of their meal. She liked this small room, how homely it felt, how easy it was just to prepare a meal and eat—rather than the impersonal feeling of a meal served to her each and every night, alone in a dining room big enough to seat twenty. Usually she brought her laptop, immersed herself in work to avoid the stark realisation that she was alone, that her mother and father had retreated to another estate far away from the palace. There was no laughter, as there had been this night, no gentle teasing or recounting of family stories, or praise of Theo's successes…and it hurt in a way she had never allowed herself to feel before.

As she glanced around the beautiful little kitchen, her eyes caught on an old black and white photo of Aggeliki and a man standing beside each other, with easy smiles and laughter in their eyes.

'Oh,' she gasped, moving towards it. 'This is such a beautiful picture of you, Aggeliki. Is this Theo's father?'

It was as if the temperature in the room had dropped.

'No. It is Nikos. We don't speak of my father. Ever.'

The words were in English, and even though she didn't think Aggeliki had translated them in her mind, Theo's reaction couldn't have been more clear. Especially when he retrieved his phone and left the kitchen.

She felt Aggeliki rub her arm softly and smile.

'It wasn't you,' she said in Greek. 'He doesn't…' She shook her head sadly, as if trying to find the words. 'He never got over it. The way his father left. I tried…to give him everything, to be everything for him. But,' she said with a shrug of her shoulder, 'he is a man. A man needs a father. For a while in Switzerland…' Sofia didn't need Aggeliki to fill in the gap—clearly her boss, the man who had paid for Theo's education, had been a father figure to him. 'But look at him now,' she said, calling Sofia back to the present, to look at him through the window. 'And look at what you both have. It is a joy to me, Sofia. *Efcharistó.*'

For the first time since they had arrived, Sofia began to wish that she hadn't come. That she hadn't seen the pain and the struggle that Theo had been through since he had been expelled from the boarding school. Because finally Theo had got his wish. She was learning about the consequences of her actions.

CHAPTER TEN

SOFIA LEANED BACK in the plush cream leather seats of Theo's private jet, hating the way that her stomach dipped and swayed with the plane. The single air stewardess made her way down the short aisle on very long legs and retrieved the empty glasses and plates from the table between her and Theo.

'Efcharistó,' she said, forcing a smile she didn't feel for the woman.

'You didn't tell me you could speak Greek,' he said, the curve of his lips a rueful smile.

'You didn't tell me that your mother had had a heart attack,' she replied, shocking them both. She hadn't meant to say the words. Hadn't meant to bring up the subject she had hardly forgotten for a moment from the night before. Hadn't meant for the smile on his lips to die away.

'No. I didn't.'

Several times, Sofia tried to let loose the

words that clogged her throat and failed. But she couldn't leave it at that. She had to know.

'Is that…was that one of the consequences you felt I needed to learn?'

He studied her, half-lidded eyes masking a whole host of emotions she desperately wanted to see the truth of.

'It was not your fault.'

'That is not what I asked.'

'I don't hold you responsible for what happened to my mother, Sofia.'

'But *did* you?'

The silence that fell between them was enough of an answer that she thought he would not speak of it again. Instead, she turned to look out of the small round window as the sprawling emerald-green stretches of Iondorran land came into view. Her country. Her home. The decisions she'd made to protect them now illuminated under the cost of her actions.

'Neither of us has had it easy, Sofia. The decisions we felt forced to make, each for other people. But this?' he said, the gesture between them drawing her gaze back to his. 'You and me? Our marriage? This is a decision that we make now, for ourselves,' he said. And she wondered at the vehemence in his tone, wondered who he might have been trying to convince…her or himself. 'It is one that I want very much,' he added, and his words soothed some of the ache that had taken up residence in her heart as he reached for her hand and drew the cool skin against the warmth of his palm.

She felt the rough calluses on his skin, marvelled at the texture as they spoke more of the hard work Theo had done than he admitted to. She knew that the fact he no longer resented her for the past should be enough, but despite the admittance she could feel a hurt emanating from him. A deeper, harder one than before.

'Do you remember my first prank? Do you remember what caused it?'

'I didn't think you needed a cause, Sofia, I thought you enjoyed playing Puck.'

'You thought me *"shrewd and knavish"*?'

'I thought you many things back then, Sofia. But yes, your first prank—on Benjamin Reneux, I remember. It was the first time that I saw you. Holding back tears of laughter as he howled in horror when he opened the door to his locker to find everything covered in honey—his blazer, his books, his homework.

You looked at me, and all I could see was you. You shone, in the dim corridor beside the Great Hall.'

Sofia nodded. 'It was not the first time I had seen you though.' She smiled, a sad smile. 'I had seen how the others treated you. How *Benjamin* treated you. The names he called you, the way even the teachers expected you to cause trouble, to be the first to throw a punch—'

'Well, I usually was the first to throw a punch…'

'No. You always threw the *second* one. I watched. I saw.'

Theo looked away as if no longer wanting to take this trip down memory lane. Unconsciously he rubbed his chest, seemingly trying to soothe an age-old ache.

'I hated it. The way they behaved towards you.'

'It was hardly less than what I had already experienced at the hands of my cousins, or…'

'Or the people who should have cared for you most.'

'Sofia, I don't want—'

'Did you ever look for your father?'

This time her name was growled on his lips like a warning.

'Do you know why he left?'

'He left because he was weak, because he was a coward who ran away from his responsibilities.'

'You were not just a responsibility.'

'What do you want me to say? That it hurt to know that my father never wanted me? That he ruined my mother and her happiness? That I swore never to be like him, only to grow into a young man who caused her more pain?'

'Is that what you think? That you caused your mother pain? That is not—'

'You know nothing of this. And I will not speak of it again.'

The gala was being held at La Sereine, a Michelin-starred hotel sitting on the edge of Lac du Peridot. As Theo leaned against the balcony looking out at the stunning sight, he tried with all his might to focus on the two large mountains in the distance meeting just at the horizon of the stunning lake, a vista of every shade of green stretching out before it. Further upstream, he'd been told, was a small town nestled around the top of a giant waterfall, feeding the river that wound its way through Iondorra to Callier.

But despite all this glory, all he could see, all he could hear were the faces and taunts of his past. He'd been shocked by Sofia's revelation—that the pranks he had so loved about her once, and then vehemently hated, had been started in retaliation against the behaviour he had received. That, all the while he'd thought to be the one who'd noticed her first, she had been there, watching him without his knowledge, and had seen him without being seen.

Somehow he felt both stunned and cheated. Cheated as if suddenly Sofia was reframing everything he thought he knew.

'Did you ever look for your father? Do you know why he left?'

He hadn't been able to answer her. Because yes, he did know why his father had left. His cousins had enjoyed taunting him with it. Older by several years, they had relished and recounted with venomous glee the story of the words he had hurled at his mother.

The story that his father had run from his mother, from the village, the same night he had been born. That he had refused to be weighed down by a child. His cousins had called him *bástardos*—bastard—for almost his entire childhood. And every time his mother had been shunned, every time his mother had been tutted at, or stared at, in the village, he knew he was the cause of it. And then later, when he had been expelled, Theo had felt as if it was happening all over again. That he had thrust shame upon his loving mother who had tried so desperately to compensate for the absence of his father, for the lack of security in their lives. So he had done everything he could, since then, to make sure that she would never feel shame or want again.

A knock sounded against the door to the suites he'd been given within the hotel, pulling him from his thoughts. A knock that sounded more like the nail on a lid that he was banging down against the memories of his father, of his childhood.

He had just walked back inside from the balcony, when he let out a bark of surprised laughter, put down the glass of whisky and greeted his friend in a warm hug.

'Sebastian! What are you doing here, my friend?' he asked.

Sebastian's grin matched his own as he explained that Sofia had arranged for him and his sister, Maria, to be in attendance for this evening's gala and for them to stay in Iondorra with Theo until the wedding. Theo poured them both drinks and, before settling down into the luxurious sofa, Theo couldn't resist one more hug. He had needed this. Had Sofia known he would? Was that why she had gathered up his closest friend and brought Seb to him?

'What is this? You getting soft on me? All this talk of romance—'

Theo laughed again, shoving at Seb before sitting down.

'Do not fear. My tastes have never run in your direction.'

'Fear? I am perfectly happy with my masculinity to appreciate another's attraction to me, no matter who it comes from. I just happen to prefer the female form.'

Theo quirked an eyebrow. 'Anyone in particular?'

'God, no. There is only one thing that would ever tempt me into the state of holy matrimony.'

'Money?'

'Amnesia.'

'I'm sure there are many women out there who would willingly oblige a good bludgeoning to ensure such a thing.'

'True. Perhaps I should start wearing a helmet.'

'A bicycle helmet?'

'Well, I was thinking something more dramatic like a knight's armour, but I suppose your suggestion would do just as well and be a hell of a lot easier to get my hands on. How have you been?' Sebastian demanded, an assessing gaze raking over Theo's features. 'You look… different.'

Theo shook off the question with a shake of his head. Sebastian was almost as close to him as his own mother, but he was not ready to open the can of worms that he'd been brooding on. Though he knew he could do with his friend's counsel. 'Honestly? I'm not so sure. Things are…different to what I had thought them to be. Sofia had her own reasons for doing what she did that night, and I… I think I understand them now.' And as he spoke the words he realised the truth of them. Theo refused to betray her confidence, even to Sebastian. But he did understand her choices, did believe her when she had said that she was sorry, and fully believed that she really did understand the consequences of her actions. And he couldn't shake the feeling that perhaps it was those very choices that had brought them to this point. This moment, where he finally had everything he'd ever wanted within his grasp.

But throughout it all was this rising sense of guilt. Guilt at what he would have done to her. Guilt for having preached all this time about the consequences of actions, when he had given little thought to anything of the consequences of his revenge. A guilt that was at once so familiar and terrible that it threatened to overwhelm him. But he could change his path. He could avoid those consequences. He *would*. This time, he could only hope that he would be good enough.

'I am going to marry her,' he said with a finality that did little to ease the feelings in his chest.

'Really?' Sebastian asked, shocked. 'I thought you might change your mind, but I didn't think you would actually get married.'

Theo shrugged off the weight on his shoulders, and Sebastian could have been forgiven for thinking that it was in response to his question.

'But I suppose it is still good business,' Sebastian said into the quiet room.

'That it may be, but no. It's more than that. It's… All these years I have thought her cold and calculating, but that's not the truth of her.'

'You love her?' Sebastian queried.

Did he? He might have been able to forgive the transgressions he thought she'd been guilty of, but love? Was he even capable of such a thing? When he thought of how he'd felt, seeing her struck by the boat's boom, when he'd paced the hospital hallways, devastated by the mere thought of her hurt, when he'd seen her share the laughter with his mother only the night before…the way it had eased a years-long ache in his chest… When he'd finally seen Sofia and how she had grown into a woman far greater than he had ever imagined possible…his lips curved into a smile, and something almost impossible to contain bloomed in his chest.

It was a strange thing, filling him from the inside out, covering and swelling to fit the empty places of his heart… Wondrous was the only word he could use to describe how it felt. And if there were edges of darkness, of a deeper hurt, of a twisted guilt in his chest, he pushed them aside with the same ruthlessness that had driven him to Sofia's doorstep.

'Yes. I do.'

'That is a wonderful thing, my friend,' Seb replied genuinely. 'Now, though, you just have to break it to my sister,' he said. 'For I believe she had pinned her hopes on the fact that you were going to abandon your princess at the altar.'

La Sereine was one of Sofia's most favourite places in Iondorra—and she had often wanted to come with Antoine, but they had never managed to find the time. She knew that being here with Theo should make her feel guilty, but she couldn't manage it. She hoped, believed, that Antoine would understand. They might not have shared everything, but they had understood each other and the pressures of duty.

Though could Sofia still claim that this wedding, this marriage, was solely for duty? She expected to feel unease as she questioned herself, but instead, she felt the thrum of excitement, of…happiness. Theo had said that he chose to do this, that he wanted it. And she was desperate to take him at his word, because somehow in the last few weeks she had begun to fall deeply for the passionate man who had woken her from a slumber of duty and grief. Her heart ached for the man she knew still hurt deep within himself. The man who had yet to resolve the real hurt that beat in his heart.

But since that night in Paris he had coaxed out some inner sense of herself—the one she had left behind with Theo that night at the boarding school—and she felt strange and new, and mysteriously whole. She felt strong…in her love for him. Because wasn't that what had really changed? That finally after all these years she had allowed herself to feel that love for him? The love that had always been there, waiting for a chance to escape, to be given to him?

With only a week before the wedding, Sofia didn't think she had enough time to undo the pain of the past, but after the wedding? Would they not have a lifetime together? For her to show him how much he meant to her, and just what he had done for her. Was it enough, perhaps, for her to do the same for him?

A knock at the door to her suite pulled Sofia's gaze from the lake and mountains beyond.

'Enter,' she commanded, her voice soft in expectation of what was about to happen. A small woman with dark hair pushed in a clothing rack with three heavy garment bags hanging from the rail.

'Your Highness,' said Alexa—her dress designer—the address slightly unfamiliar to Sofia after just a few days away from Iondorra and the formal etiquette required by her status. 'From our conversation on the phone, and the description of what you require, I have brought the original design along with some alteration options, but also two other suggestions in case they become preferable.'

'Thank you, Alexa, and thank you again for making the trip out here.'

Alexa smiled. 'It is my pleasure, Your Highness. Lac du Peridot is always a welcome sight, and La Sereine is just as beautiful as I've always heard.' Sofia couldn't help but smile at the older woman's enthusiasm. 'Now, let's see what we're dealing with.'

Sofia untied the silk robe and slipped the sleeves from her shoulders to reveal the bruise that was still quite evident from where the yacht's boom had caught her. Alexa might not have winced, but Sofia didn't miss the concern in her eyes. Alexa had been dressing and designing for her ever since she left the boarding school. She tutted as she circled Sofia with an assessing gaze. Hmmed and humphed a few times, before nodding to herself.

'You are okay?'

Sofia nodded quickly, feeling like the little seventeen-year-old Alexa had first met before her debut ball. Unaccountably she was blinking back tears and struggled to find the cause of them. She felt as if she were in a sea of emotions, her love for Theo, her hopes for the future, her ache for the past. She wanted to look beautiful on her wedding day, and the thought that had begun to wind around her heart, the possibility that the Widow Princess had finally found her Prince Charming...was one she wanted to hold on to so desperately.

'I have just the thing,' Alexa said, and Sofia lost herself in the bustling actions of the last-minute alterations to the dress she had always wanted to wear...for him.

The gala was going well. Sofia had delivered the opening speech and the event had moved on to the auction part of the evening. Theo had been with her as she had met with a few of the child ambassadors for the charity—and she couldn't help but smile at his surprise at how well she knew them. This had been her first charity, and would always have a special place in her heart. As an adult, she'd struggled with the secrecy and care around her father, so she simply couldn't imagine how much worse it was for children.

He had barely left her side all evening. And it had been both wonderful and terrible. She hadn't realised just how alone she had felt without companionship, without someone by her side since Antoine had died. Her parents had retreated to their estate, and she felt as if she had been alone for so long. But having Theo beside her made her feel stronger, more capable. It made the weight of the responsibility on her shoulders so much lighter to bear.

The thought of having him beside her in the

future made her feel more capable of the things she wanted to do for Iondorra. And for the first time, perhaps ever, she began to relish the idea of the changes, could feel the power and energy there, to do even the larger things she wanted to accomplish. Now she began to hope that they might actually weather the storm that would hit once her father's diagnosis was made public.

She cast a glance around the hotel's grand ballroom, but couldn't see where Theo was. But his absence failed to dim the thrill and excitement that had filled her when trying on the beautiful wedding dress, and suddenly the hopes for her future were almost too much for her to bear.

She looked around the room, once again, for a glimpse of the man she loved with all of her heart. She wanted to tell him. An urgency she couldn't explain began to wind within her chest. As if something, time perhaps, was running away from her.

Finally she caught sight of him on the veranda, speaking to a young woman with long dark hair that she recognised as Maria Rohan de Luen—Sebastian's young sister. They appeared to be arguing, which confused her, drawing her to the couple. The sliding floor-to-ceiling French windows were slightly open, the gauzy white curtains shifting in the breeze, doing very little to disguise their words.

'But you can't!' The hurt in Maria's voice slashed him. Theo truly hadn't realised the extent of her feelings.

'Maria, please.'

'No. You said…you said that you weren't going to go through with it. You said that you were doing it to teach her a lesson! She hurt you and you were going to leave her at the altar! You can't marry her, Theo!'

He searched his mind for explanations, something that would lessen the pain, but he didn't know what to say.

'Maria—'

His words were cut off the moment Maria's whole demeanour changed. Shocked and wide-eyed, she was no longer looking at him, but over his shoulder…and every single hair on his body lifted as if touched by the same electric lightning bolt that had struck Maria still.

Horror filled him before he'd even turned and he barely registered Maria's flight from the veranda wrapping around the ground floor of the hotel.

Sofia.

He'd never seen her look the way she did in that moment. All the lies and mistruths he'd imagined he'd seen in her features were nothing compared to the raw pain and shock vibrating from her now.

'What did she mean?'

'Sofia—'

'Is it true?' she demanded, her voice breaking over the words.

Sofia saw the moment that fear and panic truly entered him. It froze him as if he thought that should he move, should he speak, it would set into motion a chain of events he could not take back.

Finally he moved, his long legs pacing wide steps across the wooden veranda, each one feeling as if it took him further and further away from her, even as it closed the distance between them. She'd hoped, in some far corner of her heart, that Maria had lied, had misunderstood somehow. But she knew that hope was futile.

'Yes,' he said simply. And her whole world came crashing down. 'When I first met you again in Paris that night, I had a plan. I thought that I was being merciful, offering you a silent, unknown chance to apologise and release yourself of a path that would lead to your eventual humiliation. When you didn't, when you refused, I had the photographer find us in the garden—I even chose which photo he should use. And yes, when I forced your hand to agree to our engagement I knew that I wouldn't go through with the marriage. That on the day of our wedding you would be at the church filled with hundreds of guests and filmed by thousands…and I would leave you waiting as you once left me waiting.'

His voice had gained a power, a guttural tone that suggested he was almost trying to convince himself that he'd been right. That he'd been justified. Hearing the words on his lips sliced away the soft layers of her heart, until the knife struck stone.

Because that was what Sofia needed most now. A heart of stone. Because she *loved* this man. This man who would have hurt her, yes, but even worse hurt her country. The humiliation wouldn't have been hers alone to bear. It would have been theirs. And that devastated her. The one thing she had been raised and trained to do, to put her country first, and she had nearly failed even before the crown came to rest on her head.

'But I had changed my mind, Sofia. I didn't know… I didn't know about your father, about why you were forced to leave that day, about any of it. I didn't understand.'

Desperate pain filled her completely. Pain and anger, an anger that felt almost uncontainable. 'It wasn't for you to understand, Theo!' She wanted to lash out, to howl her hurt, but she couldn't. She wouldn't. Not here, with hundreds of people behind them. She had been ruthlessly trained to bear the weight of the crown and she would not betray them now by giving Theo the humiliation he had once so desperately wanted. 'But it *is* for me to protect my country and people from those who would do it harm, even those I love. *Especially* those I love. For years I have done so for my father. And now I'll do it for you.'

'But you don't have to. Sofia, I want to marry you. I want to be standing at the top of the aisle you walk down in five days' time. Sofia, I—'

'I think you've done enough, don't you? You

will have what you wanted. I will break the engagement. My humiliation will still happen for you. It will just not quite be as public as you wished.'

Theo let loose a growl. 'That is not what I want. This doesn't have to happen.'

'You think I can trust you, after this?'

'Why not? I trusted you after you…' His bitter words trailed off.

'So you still have not forgiven me. Not really.'

'I *have*,' he growled again. 'But you're leaving me, again. Just like…'

'Him,' she said, completing his sentence. Speaking of the one man that Theo refused to name. 'Is that what this is really about? Your father, not me?' She didn't wait for an answer. 'Until you forgive, Theo, you can't truly love me. Not really.'

'How on earth am I supposed to forgive him? I don't even know where he is!' he shouted.

'Not him. *You.* All this time, this unworthiness…it's you, you can't forgive, not me or him. And I can't make up for that, I can't *be* that for you.'

'Don't you dare turn this back on me. I'm

here, telling you that I love you and that I'm yours.'

'You were never mine, and you're still not,' she said, her voice barely even a whisper.

'And you're still afraid!' he accused.

'What?'

'Still afraid of letting yourself be loved for you and not *what* you are. So tell me. Who is it that really feels unworthy here? Why is it that you're so eager to fall at this first hurdle?'

'Hurdle? You're calling your plan to leave me at the altar a hurdle? The fact that you consider even doing that means you have no respect or regard for my people, my country! They *are* me and you would have left us all.'

'But I'm not! I'm not leaving you. You're the one who is walking away and if you don't see that then you're lying to yourself.'

She didn't want to hear it. Couldn't. Because deep within her heart, she knew that there was some semblance of truth to his words. But she had to. She had to leave him. Her country had to come first. Hadn't that been drilled into her as a child? As a young woman? By her parents, her father? There was no other choice here.

'I have to return to the party—'

'Let them wait!' he yelled, his voice so loud she felt it echo within her body. 'I'm trying to tell you that I love you.'

'And *I'm* trying to tell you that it doesn't matter.'

She turned to leave, but Theo blocked her path. He crowded her, his shoulders, his body a barrier that wouldn't be breached. She pulled herself up short before she crashed into him, but he caught her elbow and stopped her fall.

'I love you, Sofia,' he said, the only notice he gave her before drawing her to him, flush against his body, and kissing her with more passion and pain than she was capable of bearing. The moment his lips met hers, the fury and anger driving him, driving her, softened, and his tongue swept into her mouth as if it had a right to be there, as if it belonged to her and not him, just like his heart. Everything in her roared for release, desperate to escape and join him in this passion play. Her heart soared as much as it fell, as she realised that this would be the last time she could kiss him, hold him, show him all the huge, complex, amazing but terrible things she felt in that instant.

Her hands flew to his head, fingers riffling

through his hair, pulling him to her, as the tears escaped her eyes and rolled down her cheeks. The salty-sweet taste of them mingling with their kiss was the last thing she remembered, before pulling away from him and fleeing.

CHAPTER ELEVEN

SOFIA HADN'T STOPPED crying for two days. She hadn't left her room in Iondorra's palace, she hadn't met with the council to help create the statement that would stop the wedding in three days' time, and even her sleep was broken by huge sobs that racked her body and tears that fell down her cheeks.

From the moment she had left Theo in the hotel by the lake it had felt as if her world had shattered, and somewhere deep down she knew that she deserved it. There were things she needed to do, but her mind couldn't hold on to them. It was as if her thoughts were being filtered, all else dropping away, to leave only grief and sorrow. If she had expected numbness, a deep, quiet agony to blanket over her heart, it had not happened.

Instead she felt raw, the constant dull ache of her broken heart her only companion.

'I'm trying to tell you that I love you... You're

the one who is walking away...you're lying to yourself.'

Theo's words punctuated each breath, each thought. Because he was right. Once again, she had his heart. He loved her and she was walking away—only this time, she really was aware of what that meant. He had proclaimed to want to teach her the consequences of her actions... and now? She fully understood them.

She had been so sure in herself, so sure that she was right, putting her country first before a man who would have ruined it. Who preached consequences and gave no thought to the ones his own actions would have caused.

But beneath the words that ran around her head on a loop were the ones she didn't want to inspect. Didn't want to listen to, or believe. The ones that proclaimed her to be afraid of being loved for who she was and not *what* she was. As if the two things could be separated so easily.

This morning she had had marginally more success than the day before. She had made it to the bathroom and forced herself into the shower. Standing before the large mirror, she wiped away the steam and condensation from the cool, slick surface and stared at herself.

Her eyes, red-rimmed from the crying and a startling blue, stared back in accusation. *Coward*.

Sofia shook her head against her inner voice. No, she mentally replied. Broken-hearted.

She reached for the thick towelling robe and cinched it tight around her waist. All she wanted to do was go back to bed and pretend that the world didn't exist. She could have another day, surely. Because ten years ago, she hadn't been allowed even a minute, leaving the school and being thrust immediately into hours of lessons, measured, poked and prodded into the right dresses, as she kissed goodbye that moment out of time she'd had with Theo, kissed goodbye the young woman who had found fun and enjoyment and…love.

And four years ago, when Antoine had died, the world's press had documented her tearless grief—the loss of a man so precious to her… And for a moment she hated Theo. Hated him for showing her the truth of her relationship with Antoine—her friendship. Yes, she had loved him, but his loss had not had this devastating effect on her and somehow it made her feel as if she were betraying both men all over again.

Re-entering the suite of her rooms, she stifled a cry of shock with the back of her hand when she saw her mother standing beside the large window, looking out at the view. Shock turned into fear with lightning speed.

'Father, is he—?'

'He is fine, Sofia. He is not the one I'm worried about right now.'

Sofia's emotions seesawed, and guilt stirred in her breast. Was she so starved of love that her mother's concern—the simple fact that Sofia was being put first—made something shift in her heart? Guilt, hurt and love all mixed together in the headiest of potions, and for the first time that Sofia could remember in years she ran to her mother's arms and cried.

After what felt like hours, her mother released her and led her to the window seat.

'What are you doing here?'

'One of the staff was concerned when you refused to eat anything yesterday.'

Sofia wanted to hide, wanted to stay wrapped in her mother's arms, but knew that she could not. Slowly, haltingly, the words tumbled out. Of what had happened to Theo since she had left that night, of how he had orchestrated their engagement, but her words grew stronger as Sofia told her mother of how they had talked of the past, of the secrets she had entrusted to him, of the love she felt for him, and finally what had happened the night of the gala.

Her mother was quiet for a long while.

'Did you... Is it that you thought you couldn't have both?'

'After I left the boarding school, everything became about doing what was right for Iondorra and...'

'You didn't feel that you could have something for yourself?'

'I didn't know *how* to have both,' Sofia replied helplessly. 'It had, has, always been him. And I couldn't do that to him. I couldn't do what...'

'What was done to you.'

Sofia could hear the hurt in her mother's voice, the sheen of tears in the older woman's eyes almost too much to bear. She knew her words would hurt her mother. Knew that her mother would understand in an instant, that they had moved away from talking of Theo, and towards herself.

'Oh, my love,' her mother said, shaking her head. 'I'm so sorry that you felt that way. I... *We...*' Her words were interrupted by the shaking of her mother's head as she struggled to find the words that Sofia half feared. 'We never wanted you to feel that way. We love you dearly. And I am truly sorry that you ever felt as if you had no choice about your role.'

'I had to change so much about who I was, Mama. So much. But being with Theo again reminded me of who I once had been. And I missed that. I missed who I was.'

'And he helps you find that person you once were?'

'But it doesn't matter,' Sofia said, shrugging helplessly. 'His actions would have hurt Iondorra.'

'But they didn't, my love. And I am so happy that he brought something of you back to you. Because I have seen that smile...the one I thought lost ten years ago. I have seen what you are with him, the night of your engagement, and what you could be, in my heart's greatest hope.'

Her mother drew her into her arms again and this time Sofia let go. Let go her fears, her resentments, the part of her she thought lost, found and lost again.

'Sofia, the crown, the country, it is important. But it is not worth the sacrifice of your heart. Theo,' she sighed, a small smile curving at the corner of her mouth, 'is clearly a man who made certain choices, and although that was his plan, did you believe him when he said he no longer wanted to abandon you? Did you believe the love he said to feel for you?'

'I don't know if I can trust him, Mama.'

'Trust him with what?'

Sofia frowned, unsure of what her mother was getting at. Seeing her daughter's confusion, she pressed on. 'Trust him not to make mistakes? Sweetheart, we all make mistakes, all the time. Just look at me and your father. Do you trust him to love you and be there for you? Do you trust him with your heart?'

'But how can I trust him with Iondorra?'

'Oh, Sofia. My one wish for you is not that you have someone who puts the country first, but who puts *you* first.'

For so long, everything had been about Iondorra. Leaving school, her first marriage, even the way she had planned her second marriage. The thought that it was even possible for someone to put her first, for her to allow that... Horror and hope mixed within the chambers of her heart, rushing out through her veins and around her body, setting it on fire with adrenaline.

Could she do such a thing? Could she really give herself over to that sense of trust...of love?

For two hours after her mother had left, with promises to return more often, to make more time for the two of them, Sofia stared at her phone.

Her heart knew what she wanted to do, and Sofia waited for her mind to catch up.

She dialled his number, her heart fluttering wildly, and was almost thankful when it went to the answering machine.

'Theo, I... There is so much we need to say to each other. But more importantly, I want you to know that I love you. I really do. And if you do love me, if you can forgive me the way we parted, then I will see you at the church in three days' time. Because I want nothing more than to become your wife. I want nothing more than to stand by your side for the world to see. I want nothing more than to show the world how much I love you and want to spend the rest of my life telling you that, each and every day. If you don't come, then I understand and will not hold it against you. I will issue a statement that takes full responsibility for the end of our engagement. But no matter what, please, please know that I love you.'

Theo sat on the stairs of his mother's decking, looking out at his vineyards from the veranda. He fished the phone out from his trouser pocket and threw it behind him, and leant his elbows on his thighs. It had been two days since he'd returned to Greece from Iondorra and he hadn't slept a wink. The early morning rays from the sun heated the rain-soaked earth, covering the ground in an unworldly mist, swirling in the still morning air.

For two days he had thought of little else than Sofia, of what she had said to him, of how she had accused him of being unable and unwilling to forgive, not her, not his father, but himself. The guilt that had settled about him that night had been slowly revealed as the layers of hurt and shock from their argument had dissipated.

It was as if Sofia's words had picked at an invisible thread, wound tight around his heart—as if she had tugged on it, showing him proof that it existed, that it had bound his young heart and the muscle had grown around that binding... And he could no longer ignore it.

He had tried to lose himself in estate business, but that had failed and finally his feet had brought him to his mother's door. And although she woke early, five o'clock in the morning was perhaps a little much to be banging on her door and seeking...what? Answers? Advice? Forgiveness?

The smell of coffee hit his nose long before he detected the sound of his mother moving about in the house, and before he could get up from the wooden decking, his mother opened the door and wordlessly handed him a cup of the strong, fresh Greek coffee that he loved so much.

She went to sit beside him on the steps, and he rose in protest but she shooed him back down.

'I am not so old that I cannot sit on the steps with my son and look at the amazing things he has done. I do it even when you're not here, Theo. It is my favourite place in the world.'

Theo felt a heaviness within him. The weight of all the unanswered questions, of the guilt and anger and pain, resting on top of his already tightly bound heart...he thought he might actually break under the weight of it.

'I did something unforgivable, *mitéra*,' he said.

His mother humphed. 'There is very little in this world that is unforgivable, *yié mou*.'

He swept a hand over his face, scrubbing away the exhaustion and doubts and all the things that worked to stop his words in his throat, and opened his heart to his mother.

'I had this plan. This...act of revenge I wanted to take against Sofia for leaving me all those years ago. I blamed her for...everything. And all this time, it was me. I thought it was her fault, what happened to me at school, the expulsion, having to come back here... But those decisions and choices were mine—yet I would have humiliated her in front of the world.'

For a moment, his mother seemed to consider his words.

'But you did not.'

'Yet I would have.'

She smiled at him in the way only a mother could. 'But you did *not*.'

'The outcome will be the same. The cancelled wedding will ruin her.'

Aggeliki rocked her head from side to side as if to say maybe, maybe not, and he knew that there was only one thing to make her realise the truth of what he was feeling.

'I would have left her, just like my father left you.'

Aggeliki sighed and blew the deep breath over her coffee before sipping at the thick dark liquid. 'Theo, your father…he… I have not really spoken of him, because you never seemed to want to, or be ready to, hear of him. He was—' she let loose a little laugh '—charming—a little like his son. Very handsome—a lot like his son. But insincere and careless—*nothing* like his son.'

'Do you regret it?' *Do you regret me?*

'*Agápi mou,* no. I gave him my heart, and he gave me you. And I would do the same again and again, because you are my joy. He may have been my sadness, but *you*? You are my happiness and more precious to me than anything in the world.'

'If I hadn't been expelled I could have gone to university, and we wouldn't have had to struggle, we wouldn't have nearly lost everything when you became ill, we could have...'

'Could, would, should? Theo, you seem to think that it all would have been so easy for you had you not loved Sofia back then. But look at what you have now. Look at what you've achieved. It is impossible to say what might have happened if you had not been expelled, but it is undoubtable what *did* happen, and what you have now.'

'But we wouldn't have had to come back here. You wouldn't have had to feel beholden to your family, the cruelty and prejudice you experienced... And then with the vineyard... The hours, days, weeks, *years* of hard work—'

'I wouldn't change a thing. Life is not meant to be easy, Theo. Easy is...nothing,' she said, throwing her hands up as if throwing around air. 'Meaningless. It is the hard work that makes it all the more precious and wondrous. It is the difficult times, the sacrifices that make the joy all the more valuable, the *love*. And every sacrifice you *think* I've made? I would do it again and again, because I love you.'

'But Sofia is right. I would have brought humiliation not just to her but her country.'

'But you did not,' his mother repeated with much more emphasis than before.

'All this time, all I have thought about is myself, the vengeance I wanted, the debt *I* felt *she* owed.'

'Theo, from what I saw of Sofia, of the truly brave and powerful woman I met, she carries that burden herself. And will always carry that burden. But it is for *her* to do. You? You are the only one who can help her. The Sofia that you fell in love with ten years ago, and the Sofia that is the woman she has become. Yes, she may have to think of her country first…but you? You get to think of her first.'

He felt his mother's words deep within his chest. He felt her acceptance of his sins, his mistakes, ease some of the guilt in his heart. Soothe the way towards his own forgiveness for himself. Not for his attempt at revenge, but something deeper. But was it enough?

Theo stood and rolled his shoulders, flexing the ache from his muscles before placing a kiss on his mother's cheek.

'I need some time to think.'

Aggeliki nodded in response.

'Maybe I'll go and see Sebastian for a few days, but I'll be back. Soon, I promise. I love you,' he said, placing one last kiss on Aggeliki's forehead before walking back to the estate through the miles of vineyards between the two buildings.

Within minutes he was too far from his mother's house to hear his phone vibrate with an incoming call, and within hours the phone's battery had died, long before Theo returned to retrieve Sofia's voicemail.

What on earth had she been thinking?

As Sofia stood tucked behind the door at the back of a church packed full of nearly eight hundred of the world's leading figures, she couldn't stop the tremors that had taken over her body. Was this how Theo had felt that night ten years ago? Hopeful that she would arrive and fearful that she wouldn't?

She cast a quick glance to where her assistant was peering through a small sliver of space in the doorway, watching for Theo's arrival at the wedding that Sofia had never cancelled. The scared look in the young woman's eyes enough to tell her that Theo was still not there.

She had sent her father back to sit with her mother, after kind, coherent words of love had eased an age-old ache, but not this fresh one. And this time she had not batted her father's words away, but really listened, taken them to her heart and held them to her as if something astounding and precious.

She tried to take a breath, but the tightly corseted white satin dress just didn't expand enough to allow for it. Her hold on the exquisite garland of flowers, peonies and thistles, had become looser and looser as time had worn on, and they now hung from her listless arms at her side. The smile she had worn with determination hours before was rapidly losing its brilliance as Sofia now became convinced that he wasn't coming.

The ache in her heart was devastating, but she refused to cower beneath the pain. If this was his decision, then she would bear it. Her country would bear her mistakes too. But they would survive. This wedding, this marriage, it had been for her. The one thing she had selfishly wanted all those years ago, and again now.

But she knew that no matter what the future held, all she needed to do was put one foot in front of the other. And if that was down an aisle to tell her guests that the wedding was off, then she would do so.

She couldn't blame Theo. She understood the pain she had caused, and the hurt he felt not only from her actions, but also from his father's. Forgiveness was already there, in her heart, because she understood him, and loved him. Even if she never got to utter the words to him in person.

She gave a final nod to her assistant, who disappeared to instruct the organist not to play the wedding march as she opened the door and began to make her way down the aisle.

The unsettled and deeply curious guests all turned to watch her as she took her first step, her second and a third. Already aware that something was off, in the silence, Sofia's heart sounded in her ears like a drum.

She willed away the tears that threatened to fall. She did not want to share them with these people. She would hold them to her in the dark-est of nights, but not let them fall here, beneath the streams of sunlight falling through the stained-glass windows.

As she reached the top of the aisle where the priest stood, but the groom did not, she turned. Her mother's sad smile, encouraging and understanding, was full of love and that was all Sofia needed.

She took a breath, ready with the words she had prepared just in case...

The sound of the large wooden door being pulled open with a force that screeched across its hinges cut through the silence and there, cast in shadow amongst the brilliant rays of sunshine, was Theo Tersi.

The open promise of love shining bright in his eyes was what she'd longed to see and a sob of joy escaped her, the smile no longer forced, but came to her lips without hesitation. He took proud, deep and quick steps towards her, perhaps a little unceremoniously, closing the gap between them in moments, pulling her close and into a passionate kiss full of love and joy, much to the twittering giggles from the church's many guests.

'I'm sorry I'm late,' he said in between delicate presses of his lips to hers.

'I thought you might not come.'

'I will *always* come for you.' He whispered the vow into her ear and her heart.

Theo pulled her close to him, her heart beating against his, through the layers of clothing and skin. Only then did he allow himself to breathe. He had returned to his mother's house only the day before, and listened to the message Sofia had left on his voicemail and left almost immediately, breaking every speed-limit law in two countries to get to his future bride.

The wild beating of his heart, caused from his desperate run to the church, showed no signs of slowing. And he knew that nothing would prevent it other than the words of love he longed to hear from Sofia in person.

For the second time that day the church's doors were thrown open and Sebastian launched himself through the doors, to find the entire church staring at him. With a half laugh, half gasp, he bent double, his hands on his knees, dragging in giant lungful's of air into his chest, causing even more laughter amongst the guests than the kiss Theo had shared with Sofia.

'We would have been here sooner, but it

seems there is a no-fly zone over the church and we had to leave the helicopter about a mile away.'

'*Two* miles,' groaned Sebastian as he came to join them at the top of the aisle.

As the priest called for silence and calm, drew the guests to their role of witnesses to the marriage between Sofia and Theo, neither the bride nor groom paid heed to the ceremony, lost to each other and the love that shimmered between them. But before the priest began the vows, Sofia interrupted him.

'I have my own vows,' she whispered to the priest. 'If that is okay?' He gestured for her to continue.

Sofia took Theo's hand in hers.

'Theo, when we first met, you didn't know my title, you didn't know me as a princess, you simply knew me. You loved that person and gave her a happiness, joy and love that she had never known before. I lost a little of myself when I—' she nodded, holding back the tears '—when I left you that day ten years ago. A piece that I never thought I would get back. But in the last few weeks you uncovered that lost part of me, you showed me that I could be and have both parts of the life I so desperately wanted. And that piece was you. You were the first man I ever loved, and will be the last and only man I want by my side, whatever comes next. I want to share my joys, my heartaches and my future with you, every day.

'There are promises that I could make, some that I could struggle to keep, but the only important one is that, although I might be Queen one day, and although I will wear the crown and must think of my country first...it is our love that I will *put* first, because *that* is what gives me the strength to be Queen, to be me to the best of my ability. My love for you. My heart has, and always will be, yours.'

And as she spoke the words of her heart, Theo felt a rightness settle about his shoulders. And for the first time in so many years he finally felt whole, just as she had described.

'Sofia, you know better than most how hard the past ten years have been for me. I used to wish it had been another way. An easier way. But a very wise woman recently told me that nothing in life that is meaningful is easy. And now I wouldn't take each and every one of those hard days back for the world. Because they led me to you.

'I don't have fancy words to describe my love for you. I have only the truth in my heart, that lets me know that you are, and always have been, the only woman I would give everything for. The hard days and the good. Because you have always seen me, the truth of me, and loved me in spite of my flaws, in spite of my actions and in spite of the consequences. And I promise you here today, with *eight hundred* witnesses—' Theo paused, letting the gentle laughter of the congregation flow over the outpouring of love he felt for Sofia in his heart, before he continued '—I promise to love you, to hold you to me when things are not easy, to hold you to me when you need strength and when I do, and to hold you when we need nothing more than each other. Because you are my strength, my love and my heart.'

The truth of his words settled into the tears that pressed against his eyelids, and barely had the words left the priest's mouth declaring that he could finally, *finally*, kiss his wife, he poured his heart and soul into the kiss that would seal their marriage.

* * *

That evening, Sofia and Theo danced their first dance as man and wife to 'At Last' in front of the guests gathered for the evening's reception. The words of the song wound around their hearts as the cheers and joy of the entire room welled up around them. That night they made love, so heartfelt and poignant it felt like a dream, and it was the night they conceived their first child. Through the years to come, there would be tears of joy at the birth of their daughter, and later their son. There would be sleepless nights as Iondorra weathered the difficult revelation of Sofia's father's dementia, but there were early nights when as a family they came together to share their love. There would be tears of grief and sadness as their parents passed, but throughout it all they held each other close, whispering words of love and comfort that settled the beating of their hearts each and every single day they would share together.

* * * * *

LET'S TALK

Romance

For exclusive extracts, competitions
and special offers, find us online:

f facebook.com/millsandboon

⊙ @millsandboonuk

𝕏 @millsandboon

Or get in touch on 0844 844 1351*

For all the latest titles coming soon,
visit millsandboon.co.uk/nextmonth